BLURB

Chelsea Lawson is a ride-or-die friend. When her best friend Tilly asked her to stay at her place to watch her six-year-old daughter and pets for a while, Chelsea didn't hesitate to say yes. What she didn't realize was that "Tilly's place" was a micro-farm and "a few pets" included a cow and two goats as well as a child who was too smart for her own good.

Chelsea was already in over her head before the dead body turned up.

When the local community, instead of offering support, tries to run her out of town, Chelsea suspects something is going on. Something big and rotten. The mayor makes it clear she's not wanted and the townspeople give her the cold shoulder, but that only makes Chelsea more determined to uncover their secrets.

But no one expected the repercussions those secrets would have, especially Chelsea. Now life on the farm is hanging in the balance. Will Chelsea ever be able to wake up from this nightmare?

MOOVED TO MURDER

CEECEE JAMES

For my family, my own personal zoo. Love you to the mooon and back!

CONTENTS

Chapter 1   1

Chapter 2   10

Chapter 3   16

Chapter 4   23

Chapter 5   29

Chapter 6   36

Chapter 7   46

Chapter 8   56

Chapter 9   65

Chapter 10   72

Chapter 11   79

Chapter 12   85

Chapter 13   92

Chapter 14   98

Chapter 15   109

Chapter 16   115

Chapter 17   119

Chapter 18   129

Chapter 19   137

Chapter 20   143

Chapter 21   153

Chapter 22   160

Chapter 23   167

Chapter 24   174

Chapter 25   184

Chapter 26   194

CHAPTER 1

I've had a recurring dream ever since I was a little girl. I actually don't know when it first started. The dream has always been a part of me, ingrained in my physical body like my hands, feet and arms. I don't remember what life is like without it.

In it, I'm walking down a dirt road. It's just me, Chelsea Lawson, no-one else, and it's hot outside, the kind of heat that makes everything appear framed with a shimmer. A scorcher that drives everyone who's outside, man and animal, to search for some sort of shade, and when even a sliver is located, you'll stand, panting, wishing you didn't have to breathe.

In this particular dream, I am forced to walk. The air is filled with a heavy scent of strawberries, and the road stretches far ahead of me, the end hidden in a cascade of mirages. I have no idea what's waiting at the end. There's a feeling inside me that I'll know it when I get there.

The road is lined with street signs. As I pass the first sign, I try to read it, and that's when the dream turns nightmarish. Panic hits me, and I start to run.

It's soon after this that I wake up. Usually, I'm twisted in the sheets, sweating as my heart hammers against my ribs.

The funny thing is I'm not sure what's in the dream that has me so scared. There's nothing that hints at danger. Just a long dirt road lined with street signs.

And strawberries.

But the dream haunts me just the same. And with it comes a vague feeling that I know the place, that I should remember. That I need to remember. Yet as hard as I try, I never can.

Mom sent me to counseling back when I was in middle school in hope that I would finally be able to resolve it. I think she was tired of hearing me cry out in the middle of the night. And it must have helped because I've rarely had the dream since.

But I had it this morning. As I lay in bed, heart pounding, nothing looked familiar. I tried to place where I was. Blue curtains, quilt. And a creepy feeling that someone was staring at me.

A heavy exhale shuddered from the left. I jerked my gaze in that direction and clutched my blankets tighter to my chest. At the end of the bed, a six-year-old girl stood leaning against the footboard. She had shoulder-length mousy brown hair, awfully similar to mine, and a sprinkle of freckles.

"Hi!" she said when she caught my gaze. Casually, she swung by one hand from the bed post, the silver stars on her pajamas winking from the light escaping through the cracked window blinds.

"Emma! Hi. Wow, is it early!" I rubbed my eyes and stretched and tried to pull myself together.

Emma was my friend Tilly's daughter. Matilda Miller was Tilly's full name, but we'd met in Kindergarten more than twenty years ago, and I'd immediately shortened it to Tilly. In return, she'd split her chocolate cupcake with me. We've been best friends ever since.

We used to do everything together. Then, as adults, life happened, and we'd gone our separate ways, her to a marriage and then a divorce, and me to college and then to a very boring job with an accounting firm in Charlotte, never even moving out of the city we grew up in.

Of course, we talked on the phone, and no matter how much time passed, we always managed to pick right back up from where we left off. That was a mark of a true friend, in my opinion, when you could talk to a person like they were there all along.

It was why I responded the way I did two weeks ago when she phoned in a panic. "Chelz!" That's what she called me. My name didn't shorten nearly as cute as hers. "I'm so glad you answered."

"What's the matter?" I asked, worry filling me.

"Chelsea, I need your help."

It turned out the kind of help she needed was for someone to stay with her daughter and to take care of what she termed were a few "pets" while she flew to Australia for her first ever photo shoot. Ever since her divorce she'd been trying to get back into photography and this was her big chance. Her ex-husband was great, but as an airline pilot he couldn't watch Emma.

I, of course, agreed right away. I was due for vacation, which they didn't want to grant despite it being my first, so I actually ended up putting in my notice. After all, I could always get another job, and I wasn't sure how long Tilly might need me for. Which is how I found myself here in Cedar Falls, North Carolina with a deep bruise on my leg and a first grader staring at me.

How did I get the bruise, you might ask? Oh, that was from one of Tilly's little pets, a cow named Rosy, who kicked me instead of going into her stall for the evening. Yes, you read that right. A cow. And she had horns. Apparently all Holsteins do. The entire menagerie included her, a couple of goats, two rabbits, a cat and a dog. I didn't know how I got myself talked into these things, other than I had this not so healthy drive to help people, and I couldn't say no. But this was no time for deep introspection.

I eyed Emma now. "What are you doing up so early?"

"Watching you."

"What are you watching me for?"

"I wanted to see what an old person looked like so I can draw them." She lifted a notepad. "See?"

On the paper was a stick figure of a person with Xs for eyes and a frowny mouth with a squiggle. My shoulder-length hair was indicated with straight lines sticking out from the head like porcupine quills.

"Lovely," I breathed. "What's that by the mouth?"

"Drool." she answered simply.

I flopped back to the pillow and asked myself once again what had I gotten myself into. Not for the last time!

"How long have you been sitting there?"

"Oh, ages."

Had she heard me cry out from the dream? "Aren't there some cartoons or something on?"

"We don't get TV."

No TV? How was I suppose to watch my Housewives shows? I groaned. "Did you wake me for a reason?"

"Yes. Did you know there's a dead body in the barn?"

I bolted up like I'd been stuck with a pin. "A dead body?"

"A dead person. With Freckles."

"Who's Freckles?"

"He's the ghost that lives in there too."

Okay, no worries. This was a case of a kid with an overactive imagination.

Emma hopped up, jostling the bed, and crawled over to my side. She reached for my hand and yanked. I swear three of my fingers popped. "Come on," she insisted.

"Ow! Be careful." I snatched back my hand and shook it. "Come on, what?"

"You have to see it. Poor Freckles might get scared being out there all alone." She grabbed my hand again and pulled harder.

She was not going to give up. "All right. All right. Give me a second. Go on and wait outside."

"I know how that works. I'm six, you know."

"How what works?"

"I wait outside and then you fall back to sleep. Mommy does it all the time. But come on. I need you."

I pushed back the covers and sat up. "Let me get dressed. You too. I'll meet you in the hall in a minute. I promise I'm coming."

Reluctantly, Emma left, with me shooing her one last time at the doorway when she turned to give me another beseeching glance.

The door finally closed. I groaned and rubbed my eyes, then slowly rolled to the side of the bed and stood. I call it standing, but my spine was more like a curved bow as every muscle in my body screamed. Just one night of taking care of the cow and the goats had done this to me.

I tried to stretch it out, but it wasn't having it. Grumbling, I tugged on a hoodie and slithered into a pair of sweat pants and then found my flip-flops. I ran a brush through my hair and tucked it behind my ears. My mouth tasted like a litter box, and I needed coffee. This was all too early. I yanked open the door.

Emma fell in from where she'd been leaning on the other side.

"Oh, my goodness! Are you okay?" I asked.

"Yeah. Let's go." She'd must have moved like lighting when leaving my room the first time, because she was out of her pj's and into a t-shirt and a pair of shorts. It was a cold September morning. I was going to have to get her to change.

But first let's figure out this dead body thing. And who was Freckles, anyway? What a funny name.

She clutched my hand and dragged me down the stairs and through the house.

We walked outside into crisp air and green and sunshine. So bright I squinted.

"Come on. Just this way," she urged.

"I'm coming. I'm coming," I grunted, attempting one eye open.

Rosy mooed from the field as if to spur me on, a tuft of clover hanging from her moving jaws.

The grass was wet which made me immediately regret my choice for footwear. Water seeped between my toes before I was twenty feet away from the house.

"You were already out here?" I asked, glancing at the red barn.

"Yeah. I wanted to see if Freckles knew where the cat was keeping her new kittens. But instead I saw that person." We'd reached it by now, and she yanked open the barn door and pointed with gusto.

I rolled my eyes, ready to break into a spiel about how

7

imaginations were lovely but we had to use them for good and not for....

There was a dead body on the floor.

I screamed.

"I told you! I told you!" Emma danced around me delighted.

What do I do? Where's my phone? I kicked myself when I realized I'd left it in the house.

"Stay here, kid," I said as I started to jog back. Wait, what was I saying? "I mean, follow me. Come with me now! Emma! Quit poking that body with a stick!"

Emma dropped the stick and scampered after me as I reached for her hand. Together, we ran for the house. It was only as I hit the front porch that I realized I'd lost a flip-flop along the way.

Quickly, I dialed 911.

"911 here, this is Miss Betsy. What is your emergency?" a decidedly elderly voice warbled.

What in the world? Was this real?

"Hi. Uh, my name is Chelsea Lawson, and I have a dead body in the barn."

"And what is your address?"

WHAT WAS our address? I stared at Emma who'd scampered up on the kitchen stool and sat, swinging her legs. "Emma," I wheedled. "Do you know where you live?"

"Oh, Emma Miller? I'll send an officer right out."

"Okay. Thank you," I said into the phone, shocked she

knew, but relieved. But I didn't have time to think about that. Because, like a deranged bunny after the first carrot of the season, Jasper popped out the open front door and took off across the yard like he had a rocket tied to his hind quarters.

Straight toward the open barn.

CHAPTER 2

No! Mentally, I kicked myself. Why had I left the barn door open? It was like throwing out a welcome mat for him to come in and have a nice long sniff. What on earth had I been thinking?

I hung up the phone and ran out the door in a panic, screaming the dog's name. Jasper didn't respond. Now, I'm not much of an animal person, but I realized right about then that screaming might not be the best tactic to cajole a dog back when there was a dead body to smell, especially an animal who didn't know me very well.

He was fast approaching the barn's open doorway. I stooped to wheedling bribes. "Cookie!" I yelled. "Treat!"

"Try bath time," suggested Emma with a tilt of her head.

Without hesitating, I yelled, "Bath time!"

I swear that dog kicked up his feet and ran faster. I shot

Emma a look. She hid her mouth behind her hands, laughing like a loon.

Luckily, Jasper appeared to hate baths with such a passion that he must have decided he didn't want to be trapped in the barn. With grass clumps flying at his heels, he veered away and headed to the vacant area behind the building. The last I saw of him, he was a brown streak racing through the field before finally disappearing into the woods beyond.

A colorful string of words started to escape my mouth until I saw Emma watching me, her brown eyes rounded with delight. Oh, no way. I wasn't going to give her one more piece of ammunition to tattle on me with.

I stomped back to the house, locating my flip-flop along the way.

"I'm hungry," Emma announced as we hit the front porch.

Well sure. Perfect timing. Cops on their way and a dead body in the barn. Must be time for breakfast.

I stalked into the kitchen with Emma hot on my heels. After opening and shutting a few cupboards I located the bread and a glass for milk.

"Where's the toaster?" I asked Emma.

She shrugged and hopped up on the stool to watch me with her chin propped up on her hand. Her little feet thumped against the railing.

"Anywhere? No where?" I threw out.

She shrugged again. "Want to play hot and cold?"

Rolling my eyes, I started opening the cupboards again.

"Cold... colder," sang Emma helpfully.

I stepped away and moved toward the oven.

"Hot."

I raised my hand above the oven. "Cold."

She pointed a tiny finger. I followed the gesture to see a door. I approached it slowly, unsure of if this was another joke of hers. What if this was the stairwell to the basement? Or filled with bouncing balls? Who knew with her impish nature.

"Hotter! Burning hot!" she squealed.

I jerked the door open, prepared to bat off whatever might come flying out. Instead it was a rather boring pantry. I located the toaster and brought it out with a grateful grunt in her direction. Then I popped in the bread. "You want jelly?"

She shook her head. "Cinnamon and sugar."

I harrumphed. Still, she did help me find the appliance, so I set to finding the ingredients for her.

While it was toasting, I found some pain-reliever. Between the nightmare and the dead body, I was brewing up a storm of a headache. I swallowed the pills while Emma watched with interest.

"Don't ever touch these," I said. "Or you might need this." I lifted my shirt and showed her my appendix scar. I'd had it removed when I was around eight. I quickly buttered her toast and sprinkled it with the sugar and spice.

She narrowed her eyes. "I don't believe you. My mom takes the same medicine when she has a sore head. So that medicine has to be helping you."

She was a smart kid, I had to give her that. "Yeah, it's true.

These do help me. But if you take medicine when you don't need it, you can get very sick. Got it?"

Emma nodded, apparently appeased with my amended story. She jumped down from the stool and took her toast outside.

I peeked through the window to make sure she wasn't headed toward the barn and was happy to see her running in the opposite direction. I should have followed her, but I was already exhausted. She'd probably be okay, I thought. After all this was her place.

Okay. I needed to text Tilly. But should I wait until I had more information? I checked my watch. It was late there, I'd definitely be waking her.

I popped more bread in the toaster and poured a mug of coffee. But I didn't even get a chance to have a sip. There's the saying there's no rest for the wicked, and I was learning that must be true, because at that exact moment two very unrestful things happened. A cop car pulled into the driveway, and Emma began screaming at the top of her lungs.

Forget the police officer. I raced out of the house and around the corner in the direction of the panicked shrieks. There was Emma by the clothesline. She was waving her arms and kicking her legs in some weird kind of dance move.

Figures. I rolled my eyes. "Emma! Stop that right now! The police are here!"

In response, she kicked her legs higher, and her screams got louder. I glanced behind me to see the police officer get out of her car with a very curious, wary stare in my direction. "Chelsea Lawson?"

"Yes! Just one sec!" I yelled in what I hoped was a calming way, before jogging toward Emma.

I didn't get too far before I realized what was happening. Something black was dive-bombing her. She clawed at her neck.

Without thinking, I raced over and tucked her under my arm. I carried her to the side of the house. Once there, I quickly ripped off her shirt and batted at the insect. It was a hornet. It fell to the ground where I stomped on it. I spun her around but there were no more insects. However, I could see angry welts rising all across her neck. When I turned her back, I saw her cheeks had been stung as well.

"Bring her here!" the police officer called. I scooped up the crying girl and carried her back to the front of the house.

The officer had already found the hose and was running the water out onto the ground, making a black mud. She scooped up a handful and plastered it on Emma's stings.

Soon Emma looked like a polka-dotted Dalmatian. But her cries had subsided to a few snuffly sobs.

I knelt next to her and gave her a big hug. "Emma, I'm so sorry that happened. You're going to be okay."

"That h-hurt," she sobbed out, her little head resting on my shoulder.

"Aw, honey, I know. And you are so brave. Even braver than when I got my scar."

"You promise?"

"Yes, and do you know what kind of medicine we use for stings?"

She shook her head.

"Ice cream." I nodded emphatically. "Or a popsicle. And if you don't have any, then I'll go get some."

Squealing, this time in excitement, she jolted out of my arms and ran through the front door. "I know where we have some!" she called back.

I watched her disappear and then wearily rose to my feet and turned toward the officer. "Thank you for helping me."

"No problem. But you need to keep an eye on her for any swelling, especially those on her face. We're watching for an allergic reaction." Then she stuck out her hand. "Officer Kennedy. I heard you have a dead body for me."

CHAPTER 3

I rubbed my head, which felt like it was being split in two by a tornado.

The officer's eyes narrowed a bit as she waited for my answer. "Ma'am? A body?"

"Yeah, I do. It's in the barn. I can show you the way, just let me make sure Emma's settled."

I left Officer Kennedy standing at the edge of the driveway and sprinted up the steps and into the farm house. A quick search downstairs found Emma on the sofa with a movie blaring and an ice cream sandwich already dripping in her hand. I seized a dishtowel from the kitchen and covered her lap.

"How you doing?" I asked, tousling her hair.

"Watching Cinderella! I love her." she said, her eyes bright with excitement. "Look at the mice. This is my favorite part."

I grinned while I gave her a quick once-over. The welts seemed to be settling down, much to my relief. "It's a good movie. I used to love it too. When your ice cream is gone, come find me. I might have another prize for you."

I figured that would be the safest way to make sure I got to check on her again in a few minutes in case I got preoccupied.

She gave a big smile with white ice cream covered lips. I laughed.

With the scent of denied toast in the air, I returned outside. There I found Officer Kennedy walking backwards as she studied the driveway.

"Has it just been you here, today?" the officer asked, glancing at a notebook in her hand.

I nodded.

"Did anyone else show up? Maybe just to turn around in the driveway?"

I shook my head. Then again, I *had* been yanked out of bed a little reluctantly. I might not have noticed.

"Well," she continued, "I found some tracks at the entrance that don't match your car's tires."

I did a double blink. So, someone had been here recently.

She slid the pad into her front pocket. "Where's the body, Ms. Lawson?"

I pointed toward the barn. "It's right down there."

"And you believe the person is deceased?" she asked, marching in that direction.

I thought of his bulging eyes and gulped. "Yeah, I'm sure."

She led the way with me lingering a step or so behind. When she reached the barn door, she paused as if listening. Slowly, with her fingertips, she nudged it open. Her other hand dropped to the gun at her belt. Seeing that motion sent adrenaline zaps through my core.

I swallowed hard, as she scanned the interior. With a smooth gait, she walked in.

The body was obvious, still sprawled out in the center of the floor. To be honest, I was actually oddly relieved to see it there. After such a surreal morning, what with Freckles and the nightmare, I wouldn't have been surprised to see that it had walked away on its own. After all, this type of barn scene was in every zombie movie I'd ever seen.

Officer Kennedy whistled, and it did not sound good.

"What's wrong?" I asked, like there could be something worse than a dead body.

"Well, now you've done it."

"I've done what?" Alarm bells sounded in my head.

"You know who that is?" She squatted next to the body, her leathers squeaking. Frowning, she grasped his wrist to feel for his pulse.

"Someone important?" I hazard a guess.

"Someone important, all right. Try the mayor's cousin. This is Clint McDaniel. Mayor McDaniel is going to be all over this place like flies on a slice of watermelon."

I raised an eyebrow. What exactly did that mean? How many flies were normally on a slice of watermelon? Should I pack up a suitcase and take Emma out of town? What did Tilly get me into?

"I've never met either of them," I said. "I'm sure the family is going to be crushed. I'm sorry this happened."

She sighed and slowly stood up. "I have a feeling you're going to be sorrier when this is all said and done." Reaching for her shoulder mic, she called in a code.

The temperature in the barn felt like it dropped twenty degrees. That was a threat if I'd ever heard one. But why?

Just then I heard the slam of the front door. Emma was coming to find me to claim her second treat. I hurried out to meet her in the yard. Quickly, I checked over her skin. Although still polka-dotted, the horrible swelling was gone down. Pleased, I sent her back inside for a popsicle this time.

When I reentered the barn, Officer Kennedy was taking pictures. The air floated with hay particles, giving the scene an odd quality of sprinkled pixie dust. Magical dust of the nightmare kind.

"You find anything more?" I asked.

"No. The scene is surprisingly clean."

"What do you think happened?"

She licked her bottom lip. "I really can't say. Have you been here all night, Chelsea?"

I nodded.

"Anyone else here with you?"

"Just Emma."

She grunted. "You have anyone else who can verify that you stayed in the house?"

"You mean all night? I don't. I spent some time trying to get the cow into the stable, but she kicked me and kept on running. I finally gave up and had to leave her outside with her stall door open." As I talked, I filled the goats' bin with fresh pellets and let them out of their stall. The doe left slowly, but the buck jumped like he had springs for hooves. While Officer Kennedy continued to take pictures, I fed the bunnies. Rosy the cow was already in the field. The hay in her bin from the night before was gone so I assumed she must have wandered in at some point during the night.

Officer Kennedy grinned as she focused her camera. "Rosy. She's a handful."

"Oh, really? How do you know about her?" Immediately I was more wary over the fact the cow had a reputation than Officers Kennedy's questions suggesting that there might be some suspicion over me.

"You'll find out, I'm sure." She smirked, but before she could say more, her radio went off. She spoke into the mic again. "They're almost here."

"You did say there were tire tracks by the road," I said, crossing my arms. "So that proves someone else was here, regarding where I was last night."

"That's right." She spoke another code into the mic. "Thank you for reminding me. We'll see if we can get those cast. You sure you didn't see anyone lingering around here?"

I shook my head.

"There's just one very odd thing about Clint being here." She frowned at the body as if she were angry with him.

"What's that?"

"Why'd he end up here?" Her lip pursed. "Don't you worry. I aim to find out."

Sirens came blaring toward the farm. They all must have heard about the tire tracks because the cops parked down the road.

I walked back up to the house to make sure Emma was still contained and not bouncing off the ceiling from the sugar. Or worse yet, brewing up some plan to spring out at one of these cops to scare them.

I found her sitting on the couch with her face pressed against the window. She shivered with excitement when I entered, her little dotted face making her look like a mini clown. "Are they here to take that bad man away?"

"Bad man?" I asked.

"Yes. Freckles didn't like him at all."

"How do you know that?"

"Freckles told me when I found him." She turned her attention back to the window.

I swallowed hard and decided not to dig myself in any further with her invisible friend but to just answer her question. "Yes, the police are taking him away. We have to leave them alone for a bit. How are you feeling?"

"I'm good. My movie's over."

"Let's find another," I said resolutely.

After I had her settled again, I put in a call to Tilly. It was still late there, but I had to do what I had to do.

As the phone rang, the comment Officer Kennedy made

played through my head. Exactly how did the deceased man end up in the barn? That was a great question. There were those tire tracks. Had someone dropped him off, before driving away? And I'd never heard the vehicle.... was I that clueless?

I shivered at the thought of some strange man wandering around outside while I slept. I glanced out the window. The yard was swimming with blue uniforms.

There was one more statement Officer Kennedy made that I needed to consider.

She said the mayor was going to be mad at me.

CHAPTER 4

I bit my nail as I waited for her to answer. My hands were sweaty, and I was not at all excited about this phone call.

"Hello?" Tilly's sleepy but quite panicked voice answered. "Chelz, is everything okay?"

"Hi, Tilly, first of all, Emma is fine." Well, not exactly fine, with her having been stung all over and then dipped in mud, but I'd drop that bit of info later. "There is an issue, however."

"An... issue?" Her voice rose like someone squeezed her throat real hard.

"Yes. Um, I'm not sure how to tell you this, but we've discovered a person in the barn. He... he's deceased," I blurted out, feeling like a dad who yanked the child's wiggling tooth loose on the count of three.

"A person?" she said, her voice now dropped into a robotic tone.

The connection wasn't clear, and I rubbed my face. I hoped this was all getting through to her. "Yes, and he's dead," I reiterated.

There was a chunk of silence, and I stared at my phone to make sure we were still connected. We were, but there was no response. "Hello? Tilly?"

"Is this some kind of prank? Because it's two am right now and—"

"I assure you, this is no prank. The police are here right this minute."

"Oh, my gosh! I'll see if I can get a flight back."

"No. Don't worry about that yet. This could be an open and shut case or—" I swallowed hard, remembering how Officer Kennedy had said it was the mayor's cousin. Still, I didn't want to alarm my friend. "At least let's wait until the dust settles. I have everything under control right now." I knew this photo shoot was the biggest break in Tilly's entire career. If she left now, the chance would be gone forever. There was no need to panic. It was going to work out. It had to.

"Okay. Are you sure?"

"Absolutely."

Her voice dropped with worry. "How's my baby? Did she see anything?"

I gritted my teeth. This was the moment of truth. "She actually did, but you know your girl. She as excited as a one of your crazy goats. So excited, in fact, she somehow found a ground hornet. I killed it but not before it stung her a few times."

Tilly gasped.

"But don't worry. The police officer was here, and we slapped some mud on it. I've fed her popsicles and have been watching her like a hawk. She's fine and giddy as a hen again. I'm keeping her from all the action by distracting her with Cinderella."

"Cinderella and popsicles? Chelz, you really do have everything under control. I knew you had the kid skills to handle her. You both are getting along okay?"

"Super!" I said, avoiding the way Emma liked to stare me awake. "And tomorrow is school so she will be back to a regular schedule. I think we just have to push through."

"You'll keep me updated, immediately."

"I will. You want texts or phone calls?"

She made a humming sound, and I could tell she was trying to figure out the best way to navigate her spotty service. "How about texts but if I don't answer, then a call."

"You got it."

"And if there is even a whiff that I need to come back immediately, you let me know." Her voice held the same threatening tone as it had back when we were teens and I was going on a blind date.

"Of course, Tilly. Don't worry. I promise."

"I don't know what I'd do without you. Can I talk with Emma for a minute?"

"Absolutely!" I said and brought the little girl the phone. This time Emma's lips were stained bright red. "Want to say hi to your mom?"

She eagerly seized the phone and in excited giggles and run-on sentences, rattled out the story to her mom about the morning's crazy adventure. I cringed when she relayed—with big belly laughs I might add—the story of me trying to wrangle the cow into the barn the night before. I thought we could have forgone that little tidbit. Regardless, Tilly must have heard enough to reassure her that Emma was doing okay. I got the phone back to hear a very tired Tilly wish me goodbye, after she extracted out of me yet one more promise to keep her in the loop.

We hung up. It was perfect timing because walking up the pathway were two policemen. They looked grim. Seeing them brought that nasty flicker of an old memory back to my mind. I frowned for a second, knowing it was connected to my recurring dream. I squashed the memory down and hurried out the door to meet them.

It turned out they just wanted to record my official statement, which was hardly anything more detailed than me saying that I opened the barn door and stumbled onto the body. But they took careful notes and made me sign the paper before they left, seemingly satisfied.

After that, there was a flurry of activity as the emergency personnel packed everything up, including taking the poor man out in the black coroner's van. As I watched the last police car flip a u-turn and head back to town, I realized the yard was much too quiet, and had been for some time.

Where was that dog?

During all this activity, with strangers crawling all over the yard, there was nary a bark. Jasper hadn't returned from his break-away run earlier this morning.

I dropped my head into my hands and released a whimper. Was this day of problems never going to end?

There was no time to sit. I had to go find him.

The sun had risen just high enough to sit on the ridgepole of the barn. Shielding my eyes, I stared out through the field. There was the cow, meandering along the fence line. As I looked for the dog, my brain tried to problem solve what I was going to do with her tonight. What if I could never get her back into her stall?

Later, Chelsea, later. Dog first.

I strained to see beyond the waving grass and into the trees along the back. Trees I could barely see. Way down there. Waaaay down there. Excruciatingly far away for a person who didn't walk very much and had a bruised leg.

I glanced at the house and realized I needed to get Emma to come with me. I couldn't very well leave her alone in the house, not with what had just happened.

But what had happened? Did the mayor's cousin just wander into the barn to die? What if the man had been murdered, and the killer was in the woods?

I nodded. Right. Okay. I'd arm myself. I had pepper spray. It was probably all for naught since Officer Kennedy never mentioned murder. Besides, there's no way a killer would stick around this place when it was crawling with cops.

I headed back inside, checked Emma's stings and then had her dress for the walk. As I tied on my shoes and hunted for my pepper spray, I did wonder how long I was supposed to leave the mud on her. Did you just let it wear away?

I decided that was the best plan for now.

Feeling a courage I hadn't felt before, I reached for the little girl's hand, who quickly darted away. Shrugging, I followed her down the path in the direction the dog had disappeared in.

As I walked, my inner warning system sent a prickly feeling racing around my gut. My jaw clenched. Call it premonition, call it whatever, but it was warning me to be careful.

CHAPTER 5

On our search for the dog, we had to walk past the barn. I eyed Emma to see if she would have a reaction. Poor girl. What a terrible thing to have discovered a dead body at such a young age.

As I watched her, the uncomfortable feeling from the dream/nightmare prickled me again. Emma jumped up on a railroad tie that bordered where the hay was kept, her arms flung wide to keep balance, her face shining full of innocence. I realized I'd only been a couple of years older than her when the incident had happened to me.

I was a survivor of an accident that had been announced in all of the major news stations across the country. For weeks there had been a barrage of reporters, TV cameras, and microphones shoved in my face, as well as magazine interviews.

And I'd been trying to forget it ever since.

A cloud passed overhead, covering the sun. I shivered at the sudden temperature drop. Crossing my arms, I tried to pull myself together.

"Does Jasper come down here often, Emma?" I asked.

The little girl didn't answer me. Instead, she ran ahead to the apple trees. Catching a branch in her hand, she swung herself up onto a bigger tree limb. I watched her nervously as she scurried upward, not at all certain that what she was doing was safe.

I stood underneath the tree and stared up. "Can you climb down from there?"

As if to scare me more, she casually looped a leg around a thin branch and let go with her hands. "Why?"

Why? Because you are about to give me a heart attack! I could feel myself frowning like I'd taken a bite from a lime. I tried to remove the pucker off of my lips and respond calmly. "We have to find Jasper. He might be scared."

"He's not," she said adamantly. She dipped her leg back and then disappeared among the leaves. A few seconds later a small apple bounced near my feet. It had a bite mark in the thin skin, leaving little baby teeth impressions.

I nudged it with my foot and then faced upward. "Come on, Emma. Get down from there. I'm serious."

"I'm just eating some apples."

"Yeah, well that one looks pretty green, and those kind can hurt your stomach."

"Why don't you come up here and get me?"

She was taunting me. "If you don't get down right now, I'm calling your mother."

Well, that threat had power like it was woven with magical words. Grumbling, she shimmied down the trunk.

Her pockets, however, bulged suspiciously. I made her pull them inside out, and several apples clunked to the ground. Her bottom lip upturned like I'd just given away all her Christmas presents.

Geez. This pseudo parenting-gig was a lot harder than it looked. Was I ever going to win her over? Kids were such a mystery.

As if to prove my point, she then scampered ahead like nothing had happened, this time to chase a butterfly. The white insect fluttered inches above the golden grass heads. I soon discovered that walking through knee-high grass wasn't anything like they show in the movies. On the big screen, it seemed like it was all sweet-smelling and lovely, bobbing with daisies and blue wildflowers.

Instead I discovered it was itchy. And even worse, suddenly wet.

"What is that?" I pointed suspiciously to a bubbly patch clinging to one of the grass blades.

Emma came over to inspect it. "Spit bugs," she announced.

My jaw dropped, and I glanced at the woods which now seemed unfathomably far away.

"Come on, silly. They can't hurt you." This time Emma

took off like there was someone at the edge of the forest offering her a free ticket to Disneyland.

Ignoring all else, I chased after her.

I was halfway across the field, but at that huff-and-puff stage that I blame on dehydration, when I encountered the cloud of gnats. In a million black specks, they rose from the ground as if they shared a brain and zoomed straight for my face. I covered my nose with my shirt. Apparently, they liked what they saw, because no matter what I did, I couldn't get away from them.

Why did people live out here, again?

Just then I skidded in the dirt. Glancing down, I saw there was no mistaking that it was in fact a big cow patty. I almost cried, I really did. Instead, I straightened my spine, scraped my shoe against the grass—noting the spit bugs—and then ran as fast as I could to get out of Dodge.

By the time I cleared the flies, Emma had ducked under the fence and was about to disappear into the woods. I didn't have time to freak out. Instead, I ran faster.

I caught up with her just as she jumped over a fallen tree.

"You stay with me or there's no more popsicles ever." I couldn't keep using her mom as a threat forever and that was my attempt to come up with another credible one.

She shrugged, not seeming to be afraid.

"I mean there will only be cauliflower and meat for meals from now on."

She stared at me, wide eyed. "No more Noodle O's?"

"Only if you stick close to me," I warned. I tried to talk slowly like I wasn't winded from chasing after her.

That seemed to be an adequate enough threat. She fell in line with my pace. Together, we called for the dog, with me throwing out as much of an enticing tone as I could.

Nothing. We delved deeper into the forest. I threw an anxious look back but could still see the sun shining brightly through the tree trunks.

Finally, I heard something. I held up my hand and paused, trying to listen. "You hear that?"

Her lips puckered, and then she nodded. It was a dog barking.

"He's over there," I said and headed in that direction, circumventing several bushes. Behind them was another fallen tree. I held out my hand to help Emma over. She used the opportunity to walk the length of the trunk. With a satisfied grin, she jumped off and held her hands out like a gymnast.

"You stuck the landing!" I grinned back. Her hair was a frazzled bird's nest. With the way our morning had started, I'd forgotten to brush it. And with those mud splotches and stained lips, she looked like a hot mess. Still completely adorable.

"What's that mean?"

"It's what gymnasts do when they land perfectly."

"Huh." She wasn't impressed. "Jasper!"

The dog answered back with excited yips but didn't seem to be coming toward us. Was he stuck on something?

"Do you and your mom come back here often?" I asked,

slightly creeped out by how thickly the trees had closed in around us. I glanced behind and could still make out the light.

"We've never been here before."

I swallowed hard and gripped the pepper spray. What if we were about to stumble onto a bear? It was one thing for me to be here alone, but to bring a child?

I fumbled out my phone and gave it to her. "You know how to call 911?" I asked.

She nodded solemnly.

"If trouble should happen, I want you to run that way and call 911, got it? Don't worry about me." It was the best I could do. I hoped I wasn't making this kid paranoid for life, especially after the events of the morning.

"Got it," she whispered.

"Stay behind me," I said and moved forward.

The dog's barking was sharp and bold now. I expected at any moment to see the shaggy animal. We rounded the last clump of bushes and came into a grove of baby trees.

Sitting in the middle of the copse was the dog. He sat, tongue lolling out, looking as pleased as punch that we'd played his game.

"Jasper! Get over here!" I said, patting my leg. I grabbed my forehead when I realized I hadn't brought a leash.

True to his nature, instead of coming, he turned and bounded away.

"Is Jasper even his name?" I asked crossly.

"That's his name alright. Of course, Mom calls him some other ones."

"Like what?" I asked hopefully.

"Like floppy-eared turd-basket," she said with a nod. "She did that the one time when he was running away with her car keys. He likes to play tag."

I closed my eyes and whimpered. We could be here all night.

The dog barked again, teasingly. We followed after him, weaving around the slender trunks of the new trees.

This time the dog stayed as we approached. I froze in surprise. Not because the dog waited for us, but that he sat next to an old car. And by old, I mean one of the trees was growing right through the front seat.

"Oh, Chelsea! Look at this!" Emma squealed as she ran over to her dog.

I followed after her.

She hugged the dog and grinned like she'd found treasure. "Can we keep it?"

My gaze jumped between her and the interior of the car. Cautiously, I stooped to peer inside the vehicle.

The glove box was open. Spilling out from the inside and piling all over the bench seat was stacks of wet bundled money.

More money than I'd ever seen in my lifetime.

CHAPTER 6

"Emma, let me see my phone." I reached out my hand. I needed to call the police. I mean, it's not every day you see rotting bills lying everywhere.

She skipped over, one of her shoes dragging untied shoelaces through the dirt.

I took it and scrolled for Officer Kennedy and then hit send. As the phone rang, I walked around the car. The back symbol said it was a Pontiac. It was old, and the paint faded, but I saw enough to think that it was originally a grayish blue. There were no license plates.

"Officer Kennedy," she answered, her voice crisp.

"Hi. This is Chelsea. Hey, I was wandering in the woods looking for our dog, and I came across an abandoned car."

"Yeah?" Her voice rose with interest.

"Yeah. It looks like it's been here for ages."

"Oh." Disappointment made her voice plummet. "I can send someone out, but this is no priority."

"The thing is, there are piles of money all over the front seat."

"Yeah?" Up went the tone again, just like some crazy yo-yo. "I'll be right over. Meet me at your driveway."

We hung up, and I stared at the dog, trying to think of how to get him back home. Finally, I yanked my shirt over my head—making Emma giggle—and tied the arm through the collar of the dog to use as a leash. I wasn't taking any chances with Jasper disappearing again.

We headed home. Twenty minutes later, I met Officer Kennedy in the driveway, and the three of us, including Emma, headed back out across the field one more time. Poor Jasper barked at the window, heartbroken that we'd left him.

"Watch for the cow patties," I warned, keeping a sharp eye out myself.

Officer Kennedy ignored that and instead casually said, "Keep it on the down low, but preliminary blood levels show Clint most likely died of some type of tranquilizer drug overdose."

I frowned, glancing at Emma. I didn't want her to hear.

I needn't have worried. The little girl was singing and picking the last few dandelions that had braved the colder weather. I thought she was being sweet until I heard the words of the song.

In her tiny voice, "Mommy had a baby, and its head popped off." With a flick of her thumb, the flower head went flying.

I grimaced and turned back to the police officer. "Okay. So an overdose," I said.

She walked through the wet grass without even a glance at the ground. "Well, I'm telling you this because the levels were high. Too high."

"What does that mean?" I asked, even more confused. Obviously they were high. The man was dead.

"It means the toxicity was above what any normal person could administer to themselves before they passed out." Her gaze flicked toward me, and she sighed like she was disappointed I was so dense. "It means someone had to have killed him. And I'm letting you know since it happened so close to your house. Be on guard."

Geez! "Do you think it's safe to stay here?"

"I can't tell you that. But, in my opinion, I think the attack was specific to Clint. It's up to you though. I'll have an officer drive by a few times at night."

I nodded. How could I leave? There were all these animals to take care of. I had to do what I said I would do. Tilly depended on me.

We'd reached the woods by then and carefully picked our way over the fallen trees and through the saplings. She sucked in a breath when she saw the car, and I was oddly please to have finally caused her an emotional reaction. Emma ran forward to reach for one of the bills that had made its fluttery way onto a branch.

"No! Stop!" Officer Kennedy commanded. "Now!"

Emma froze, startled at the sharp voice. Her eyes puddled, and she glanced at me.

"Come here, sweetheart. It's okay," I said, reaching out a hand. And then quieter, to the officer. "She's been through a lot today, and her mom isn't around."

Officer Kennedy pulled the camera up from around her neck and began taking pictures. "You two take any of this money?"

"Are you kidding me? Of course not!" I huffed. Emma squeezed my hand.

"Don't be so touchy. No offense intended. I just wanted to know if the scene had been disturbed. Two new mysteries in one day. You're good for job security." She removed her flashlight from her belt and used it to peer inside the car. Cobwebs hung from the ceiling and the windshield was nearly obscured with algae scum.

"Huh." She walked behind the car and continued another fifty feet or so. "There's an old road back here. Must be how the vehicle got in."

I followed after her. What she called a road was overgrown with more saplings and blackberries. I glanced at her questioningly.

"Look up there." She pointed to the tops of the trees. When I glanced in that direction, a path through the tree branches was visible where they gapped.

"Okay," I said.

"Looks like this road has been abandoned for at least twenty years or more."

I nodded, but Officer Kennedy wasn't paying me any attention. "You two head back to the house. I've got this covered. I'll probably see if the officers can get down this old road." Before I could respond, she was talking on her mic.

Suitably dismissed, Emma and I walked back home. The little girl tried to break away from me once, but I firmly hung on to her hand.

She was sneaky though. At first she seemed resigned, but as soon as my attention was distracted by a fallen tree, she jerked away. Dang, that kid's hand was sweaty. "Emma!" I called.

The little girl ran through the trees.

With everything going on, I didn't want her out of my sight. I ran until I caught up with her and then scooped her in my arms. "Where do you think you're going, you little monkey?"

She dissolved into giggles, as I carried her a few more feet. At the fallen trees, I set her down and reached for her hand again. "When I tell you to stay with me, you have to stay. I'm trying to keep you safe."

Her eyes were wide as she looked up. "Okay, Chelsea. I'm sorry."

We headed back to the house where I had to give Jasper a treat to earn his forgiveness. I had no idea if I should let him outside again. What if he found his way back to the Pontiac and ran off with the police?

I was pondering that when Emma chimed in. "Momma uses the dog run sometimes, especially when we have new piglets. Jasper goes crazy for those pigs, and she's afraid the momma pig will squash him like a tater tot."

"Where's the dog run?"

She showed me, and I led Jasper there. Then I decided to do my outdoor chores. I changed the straw in the cow's stall and then filled her bin with fresh hay. There wasn't much feed left. Tilly had mentioned there would be a delivery this week, and we sure needed it. She left the number. I had to call them.

I filled the water pan for the goats. It took several trips. Wow. Tilly did this all by herself and then worked a full-time job? I had no idea how. I was already exhausted.

When the animals were situated, I headed back inside, grimy and covered with dirt and hayseed. I need to get dinner started. I was starving and poor Emma had only had ice cream and some toast. I was having a heck of a time juggling everything.

As I washed my hands, Emma began setting the table. I rummaged through the freezer for a pizza and found a box. Quickly, I opened it and threw it in the oven. It was a gas range, and I wasn't sure exactly how to use it.

I stared at the dials. "Stand back!" I told Emma.

She scooted to the doorway with a giggle. "You are funny. Freckles thinks so, too."

Yeah, well I might be sending Freckles sky high along with

everything else in the house if this went wrong. I turned the temperature on and pressed start, my every muscle tensed to spring away.

What really happened was the click of the igniter scared me so badly my legs almost gave way.

I whirled around to Emma. "Was that sound normal?"

"Uh huh. The burners make the same sound."

Okay. Everything was working like it was supposed to. I cautious moved away, after another suspicious stare. Then I turned my attention to Emma.

She smiled like a muddy little scarecrow, polka-dotted and red-stained popsicle lips.

"You need to get in the bath, little miss," I said.

"Momma says I only take one bath a week."

I frowned. "Well you have mud all over yourself, and tomorrow is school."

"I have eczema and baths make it worse." She crossed her arms, tit for tat.

The thing was, she had me. Could it be true? Maybe? Tilly hadn't mentioned anything about eczema, but then again, she hadn't mentioned that her cow liked to charge people and kick at them. "At least go wash the mud off your face. But be careful with the stings."

A cop car drove into the driveway. I hoped Emma would be cleaner when I saw her again and hurried out to the front porch.

Jasper was doing his job as a guard dog and barked at full

volume. He lunged at the end of his lead like he was ready to tear the man's throat out.

The officer glanced at the dog and then at me.

"Officer Kennedy sent me to...."

"What?" I yelled, unable to hear him over the dog.

He started again, but it was no better. Jasper was not backing down. The dog saw a stranger and wanted him gone. Pronto.

I waved the officer into the house.

He began again. "Officer Kennedy sent me to tell you we are done back there. I'm on duty tonight, and I'll be driving past your place to check on things. I'm sure you're going to be fine, but let us know if you need us in any way." He raised an eyebrow. "She also said to tell you that Rosy was in the stall so she went ahead and shut the outside gate. Everything's buttoned up for the night."

Officer Kennedy put Rosy away? I felt guilty for the relief that flooded through me. That cow was my responsibility. I couldn't let her be the boss. But at least I didn't have to worry about her tonight. "Okay, thank you very much. And thank her, too."

"We were able to get what we needed but until we remove the car, I suggest you stay away from it. It's full of rust and falling apart. It could be a danger to the little girl."

"Of course," I said, distracted. I had noticed a suspicious carbon smell. Two seconds later the fire alarm went off. "Oh, my gosh!" I yelled and ran back into the kitchen.

Smoke poured out of the vents in the oven. I turned off

the oven, threw open the window, and started fanning the air frantically with a towel.

The cop had followed me inside a few steps and glanced curiously around the house. "You sure you're okay?" At least that's what I thought he said. I couldn't hear him over the fire alarm. Jasper's barking seemed to reach a fevered pitch in competition with the alarm.

"It's nothing." I puffed and then smiled reassuringly. In my head I was begging him to go away.

He seemed to read my mind. He raised his hand in goodbye and then left, shutting the door firmly behind him.

Finally, the alarm turned off. Jasper quieted as well, except for a random yip here and there as if to remind the world he was still watching.

I wandered into the living room and collapsed on the couch, feeling utterly defeated.

Only one week. I could do this for one week. In grim defiance, I sent Tilly a text to tell her all was well and then slumped my head against the pillow.

Emma came around the corner looking fresh faced but also with a grin like she'd played a joke on me. I was too exhausted to find out.

I dragged myself from the couch and back over to the stove. There, I sadly scraped the pizza into the trash can and then searched for a couple cans of Noodle Os. At least I knew she would eat the dinner.

So far just two days in, and I felt like a complete failure

with kids, animals and cooking. But I discovered I was awfully good at finding mysteries.

And chores. I sure as heck wished I knew how to enlist Freckles to help with some of the farm work. Right about now, I'd take any help I could get.

It couldn't get any worse, right?

CHAPTER 7

The next morning the alarm went off accompanied by me sitting straight up in bed. I had had my dream again... my nightmare dream.

A scent of strawberries still seemed to linger in the air, and my heart galloped like it was trying to escape from a bony jail. The room was unfamiliar, and I clutched at the blankets.

Slowly the events and memories from over the past few days shifted into place. I slumped back to the pillow and covered my eyes.

The shiver of shadows and red splotches played behind my closed eyelids. I sucked in a breath and was surprised to feel the tickle of a tear running down my face.

I rolled over and grabbed my wallet and rifled through its contents. Finally, with a deep exhale, I found what I was looking for—a picture.

It was of me and my Mom as I sat looking at my profile in a mirror. Mom had on jeans and a flowered shirt, and although she was thinner than she is now, her mid-section suggested extra weight that she had always complained she wanted to lose. I was younger than Emma in the picture. In fact, I didn't remember the picture being taken. I had very spotty memories before the age of five. I didn't know that wasn't normal until I learned most people could remember stuff from back then.

For some reason, Mom had hated the picture when she saw it and tossed it out. It was her smile, she said, before insisting she didn't really look like that.

I'd pulled it from the trash and kept it, finally folding it to fit my wallet when I was a teenager. I needed it with me. It brought me a strange security I couldn't put into words.

I studied it now, feeling a slight comfort, before rolling over for my phone.

It rang, and I silently prayed Mom would pick up. She was in Mexico rebuilding homes for an area that had recently been destroyed by a storm. She was my rock and after I grew up and moved away, she became other people's rock.

Finally, Mom answered. In a similar way that a certain sweet scent draws out memories of childhood birthday pancakes, her voice immediately grounded me.

"Hello? Chelsea are you okay?" The phone crackled, indicating she didn't have the greatest reception.

"Hi, Mom. What are you doing?"

"Chelsea, what's wrong?"

"What do you mean, what's wrong?"

"When you call me this early, I know something is going on. I knew you shouldn't have gone out there to Cedar Falls."

I heaved in a breath. Her words nearly caused my emotions to come undone. And, just like a snowball rolling down a mountain, there would be no stopping them once they were released. I squeezed my eyes, trying to pull it together. I was always trying to pull it together. I needed to reassure her that I was okay. Except that I wasn't, not exactly. Things were falling apart.

And I'd had the dream again.

But I knew I couldn't tell her all that, especially the part about the dream. It would break her heart if she knew I was still dealing with it. She'd had such hope in her eyes when the counselor had told her I was okay. I finally quit mentioning it back in my early teens. I couldn't do that to her again, especially now that she was so busy with her own life.

"I'm fine," I lied, and purposely kept my voice light. "Just getting ready to start my day and wanted to check in with you before things got too crazy around here. I miss you, ya know."

"Oh, honey, I miss you, too. I'm so glad things are going well." Then she began again, her voice filled with suspicion. "How is Emma doing?"

"She's good, other than taking great delight in trying to torture me. Are all kids like that?"

Mom chuckled, which I could barely hear over the buzzing phone line. "Every single one of them that I know."

Since I was an only child, I knew exactly who she was shading. "Aww, come on. I was a great kid!"

"Great, huh? What about the time you spray painted the cat's tail?"

I cringed. "I was trying to mark him so the neighbors knew he was ours! They kept saying they had feral cats on their property."

"All I know is that poor cat had a blue tail for the longest time. And what about the times I used to send you outside to play and you'd sneak back in through your window to play your video games?"

Okay. Maybe I wasn't so great.

Just then a low moo carried through the air from the barn. I glanced out the window, my every muscle screaming in protest at the sound. It was a misty cool morning, and rain drops from a storm during the night clung to the window screen. I needed to get up and get things ready.

"Well, Mom, I can't tell you how good it is to hear your voice. I wish I could talk longer, but I've got to get going."

"Okay, love. You have a good day and don't wait so long to call me again, you hear?"

I promised her. "I love you bunches and bunches," I said, finishing with our usual saying.

"Toasted honey bunches," she shot back. "I'll be in the city soon, and we can talk longer."

I grinned as I hung up. Then, after running my finger over the picture one more time, I folded it back up and returned it to my wallet.

I walked over to the suitcase and pulled out a shirt. After a smell test, I threw it on, along with some pants. Then I ran downstairs to put cereal, milk and a bowl out on the table. Emma still wasn't knocking around yet. In fact, I hadn't even heard a peep from her room. Not good for the first day of school and my responsibility to get her there. I pounded back up the stairs and knocked on the door.

"Just a minute!" she called. "I'm getting dressed."

"Your breakfast is on the table," I hollered. I waited a moment to listen. When there was no response, I headed back downstairs. My legs reminded me on each step that I'd skipped leg day. Apparently, for the last twenty years.

They were getting some use now. At the foyer, I tugged on my boots and shrugged into my jacket. "Hurry up, Emma!" I yelled again, and then headed out to the barn.

The air was frosty with the rising morning fog and smelled of sweet hay. But I wasn't feeling peaceful. In fact, I squeezed my hands so tightly that my nails bit tiny crescents into my palm. My brain warned me to be careful of what I could find this time. I stood before the barn door. Count of three. Come on. Let's do this.

The cow mooed again, insistently. She wanted food, and she wanted it fast. Before I could count to three, my instincts kicked in. I swung the barn door open, like ripping a bandaid off.

Warm straw-scented air and a bunch of blinking eyes greeted me.

I took care of the goats first. They were insistent and their bleating was nearly deafening. I opened their side door, and they about knocked me over to say hi. The buck lifted his lip and bleated a hello before scampering out the door. Daisy, the other one, butted up against my hand a few times, very insistent for some more attention. I rubbed her ears and face and then nudged her to one side so that I could fill their troughs with water and pellets. Then I ran for the wheelbarrow and pitchfork to clean the pen.

That finished, I trundled the dirty bedding out the back of the barn door to the refuse pile and then brought in fresh straw.

After spreading it around in the goat pen, I shut the stall door and stared at the one on the other side. There was no more delaying it. It was time to start on the cow.

I approached Rosy a little apprehensively. Her eyes were large and wide as she regarded me in return. I needed her to scoot back so I could get in her stall and open her gate. I took a step closer and reached for the stall door.

"Mooooo!" she hollered, shaking her head and letting me get a good look at her horns. I squealed and tripped backwards. Good grief, I needed to get a grip! Cows do moo!

Feeling a little more forceful, I approached the cow's stall again. "That's enough of that, Rosy. You have to scoot back. You want your breakfast, don't you?"

She did a double long blink, lifting puppet-length white eyelashes, but otherwise didn't move diddly squat. I reached over the fence and tried to nudge her shoulder.

It was like pushing against a furry brick wall. Frustrated, I tried to assess the situation. The cow wasn't going to move. Yet, I still had to somehow open her outside gate.

A brilliant idea hit me. I seized a rake. Carefully, I rested the metal prongs on the stall door and eased the handle past her, aiming for the latch on her gate. I wiggled it, standing on my toes, my arms screaming as I struggled to reach.

Almost there. Almost there.

Finally, the latch dropped, and the door swung open. Rosy turned toward the sunlight and slowly lumbered in that direction out to the field. Moving fast, I opened the stall door and shut the gate behind her.

She was out! Heaving a sigh of relief, I grabbed the pitchfork and started scooping out the used straw into the wheelbarrow. After dumping it and freshening her bed, I fed the bunnies, and then walked over to the hay bales under the shed roof.

It was time to load the outside feeder. There was only a half of a bale left. In all the commotion yesterday, I'd forgotten that I'd meant to call the feed store about the delivery.

I loaded the remaining hay into the wheelbarrow, and, with heaves and grunting, I trundled it to the metal feeding cage. Rosy met me as I forked the hay over the fence and into the cage. She pulled off a tuft while I was sweating buckets and feeling as weak as a wet paper bag. I still had to fill the watering trough. Thankfully, this one had a spigot that ran right into the metal tub.

I reached through the fence and turned it on, listening to

the splashing sound of it pooling in. As it filled, I leaned against the fence, trying to look like a professional farm girl. In reality, I was hanging onto the fence so I didn't topple over.

Rosy tore another mouthful off and munched thoughtfully, stray hay blades moving into her mouth bite-by-bite like stiff spaghetti. We stared at each other, she and I. She was clearly unimpressed with my farm girl act. Finally, I was able to turn the water off and wearily head back inside.

I walked into the kitchen to discover Emma sitting at the table scarfing down a bowl of cereal. There was a piece of toast popped out of the toaster and waiting to be buttered. The sight of her up and eating should have pleased me except for the large orange towel wrapped around her head.

"What's that?" I asked, after washing my hands. I poured myself a mug of coffee. I needed to drink a gallon to have any chance of regrouping here.

"Hair's wet," she said, not taking her eyes off of the cartoon movie which could be seen playing on the TV in the other room.

"Why's it wet?" I took a scalding sip and nearly spit it out.

"Washed it."

I frowned as I wiped my mouth. "You took a shower?"

She shrugged, eyes still glued to the mouse being chased by a cat. I leaned over and pulled on the towel.

Wet bluish hair cascaded out. I gasped. "Emma! What did you do?"

"Colored it," she said simply. She had the decency to look a little nervous this time.

"I can see that. What did you use?"

"My soccer hair dye."

"Go get it," I demanded.

She rolled her eyes but trudged to the pantry where the trash can was kept. Rifling sounds could be heard. Moments later, she came out carrying a dripping container.

I rushed over to retrieve it from her and held it over the sink to read. "Good for eight washes!" it screamed from inside a star icon.

Well, the good news was that it wasn't permanent. The bad news was that there was a bus coming in about ten minutes. Exactly how long did a hair wash have to be to count as one?

"Get over here," I said, bringing her to the sink. She couldn't reach the faucet so I dragged a chair to the counter. She knelt on it while I ran warm water over her hair.

Blue did go down the drain, but not enough. I grabbed the closest thing, dish soap, and squeezed some in my hand. Did people use this stuff in kid's hair? I shrugged. It *was* soap. I was desperate, so I scrubbed.

Her hair was soon hidden under a thick blue lather. The clock on the wall ticked, stressing me out. I rinsed her hair, only to discover it was just as vibrant as ever.

Even worse, my hands were now blue as well.

"Mother of a Sunday biscuit!" I yelled. I snatched up a towel and gave her the quickest toweling down possible. Then after another panicked glance at the clock, I carried her into the bathroom where I plied exactly two minutes fifteen seconds worth of hair dryer heat. Finally, I brushed her hair as fast as possible while trying not to hurt her, and then scooped it back into a ballerina twisted bun.

One more feverish glance at the clock had me grabbing her jacket and her hand, and my purse. We ran down the driveway where I could see the bus approaching in a cloud of dust.

"Here, take this," I said, sliding out a ten dollar bill from my wallet. I had no idea if it was enough for lunch but I hoped so.

"Cool!" she said, her eyes bright with excitement. "And I'll swap you this!" She pressed something in my hand.

"What is it?" I stared down curiously.

The bus rumbled up, and the door opened with a hiss and a clang.

"It's something I found in the field yesterday!" she shouted, before bounding up the metal stairs.

I watched with my mouth hanging open before vaguely waving as the bus lumbered out of sight, carrying the blue-haired sprite with it.

Now what was this weird thing she'd given me?

CHAPTER 8

I t was a weird heavy hook. But in studying it, my blue hands popped out like neon signs, reminding me that I had an interview later. I scrubbed them, even using the plastic scour pad. But the action of having completely dried seemed to make the stain deep set because it wasn't budging.

Sighing, I grabbed my phone and searched for the number for the feed store. While it rang, I reached for the hook and rolled it over in my hands.

"Hello? Farm and Feed. How can I help you?"

"Uh, yeah. I'm staying out at Tilly Miller's place, and we were supposed to get a load of alfalfa hay. It never showed up, and I've pretty much run out."

"Oh, how strange. Just one moment." I was placed on hold to be treated to a fabulous selection of elevator music. My stomach churned from hunger, and I reached for the piece of the now cold toast from the toaster. Chewing it reminded me of a piece of leather. I popped in a fresh piece of bread, noting the dark circles under my nails. Nails that had once been carefully manicured. I pinned the phone down against my shoulder as I fished the butter and jelly from the fridge, contemplating my new life as a farm girl.

The lady returned. "I'm sorry. It shows that it was delivered yesterday morning."

My toast came up, but I didn't grab it. "Uh, no one showed up from the Farm and Feed. Of course, we had a really strange day yesterday."

"Actually, it seems to be kind of strange here as well. I wish I could ask him, but our delivery guy hasn't shown up to work today."

"Really? What time was he supposed to be at my place?" I asked, pacing. Behind me, like a shaggy shadow, Jasper stayed at my heels. His nails clicked with every step.

"Deliveries that small are usually handled by personal trucks. They loaded it in, and he was supposed to be at your place around six am."

A suspicion grew inside. "And you can't reach him?" Was their delivery guy Clint?

"No ma'am. I just found out that Micky's been trying to reach Sam on the radio all morning."

"Who's Sam? Is that the delivery guy's name? Could he have gotten lost?" The dog's sad eyes found mine and latched on to the toaster. I realized he needed breakfast as well. I picked the toast out and broke him off a piece. He snapped it out of the thin air. Poor boy. I headed into the mud room to fill his dish with kibble. He gobbled it down like it was prime rib.

The woman answered, "There's no way he could have gotten lost. Sam's been out to your place many times. Talks about Jasper all the time."

So it wasn't Clint.

"I'm still not sure what happened, but we can drop off an emergency load of feed today." Her words were reassuring but her voice was full of concern.

"Thank you. That'd be a great help. I hope you find Sam soon." I ended the call and took a bite out of yet another piece of cold toast. Should I call Officer Kennedy and let her know that our scheduled delivery never showed up? And what about the hook that Emma found. Was it related?

Sighing, I left the message for Officer Kennedy. I wasn't sure if it wasn't just a coincidence and I was leading her down a rabbit trail. But then again, I wasn't sure how my hands were still blue. I just had to do the best I could.

I glanced at the clock as I shoved the last corner of the toast in. Good grief, where had the time gone? I had a job interview in less than an hour. I led Jasper outside and attached him to the lead for a potty break. He'd be alone in the house until I could return at lunch time. I hoped he wouldn't destroy anything.

I hopped in the shower where I tried to scrub my hands

again. It wasn't helping a bit. I resigned myself to keeping them stuffed in my pockets during the interview.

And, just like that, it was time to go. The house was a disaster. Scattered breakfast dishes, toaster surrounded by crumbs, dog hair floating in the air. The walls were closing in on me. I needed to get out of here. I brought Jasper back in where he promptly jumped on the couch to watch me leave from the window.

I waved and blew him a kiss, and then left for my next adventure.

AFTER ALL OF THAT, I ENDED UP HAVING ABOUT TWENTY minutes to kill before the interview. The toast hadn't been near enough, so I stopped at Sweet Buns Bakery. I grinned a little wryly at the name. Pastries sure didn't help my buns, but it would be nice if they did.

The place was charming with a striped awning rippling in the breeze over two small table and chairs. The bakery's display window held what appeared to be a scarecrow, complete with straw poking from his shirt sleeves. I paused outside the window and was surprised to see it was a cake. Everything was covered in frosting or fondant, included the leaf-shaped cookies at the scarecrow's feet.

Clever. I gave my reflection a once over and noticed a good-looking man behind the counter watching me.

With a smile, I opened the door. "Hello, there!"

"Morning!" he answered and leaned on the counter, his sleeves rolled to expose muscular forearms. "What can I get you?"

I stared at the menu board on the wall behind him, a little overwhelmed.

"Uh... " I hummed, probably sounding like a doofus. Why was it so hard to decide? Coffee? Gee, never had coffee before. "A medium Americano, please," I finally ordered.

"Sure thing. You want a snickerdoodle to go with it? I just pulled them out of the oven a few minutes ago."

A man who makes coffee and bakes too. I had to introduce Tilly, she'd love him. My attention dropped to the glass counter case where sugar-encrusted golden piles of goodness called my name. My mind argued with my heart for a nanosecond, but the heart wants what it wants.

"Those are gorgeous. I have to try one."

"Sure thing. You're not going to regret it." He plucked at his collar like it itched.

"You made these?" I asked.

"Yeah. This is my place. By the way, I'm Tom. Here or to go?"

"Here," I said. He nodded and snagged a mug from a stand and held it under the coffee machine to fill. "So who made those," I pointed to a tray of glistening baklava.

"That would also be me." He grinned, eyes twinkling.

"Oh, seriously!" I said. Tilly was going to be over the moon.

"Don't sound so surprised. That's actually my

grandmother's recipe, passed down to her from her mother. You've got to try it."

He was maybe a little younger than me, somewhere in his mid-twenties, and I was surprised to hear he baked. That's a horrible thing to say. But I was.

Tom placed the cup on the counter and then grabbed the cookie with a wax napkin and set it on a plate. I fished out my debit card and cringed slightly as I passed it over with my blue paw.

He didn't say anything, but the corner of his lip tugged up more. He rang the purchase while I strived to explain. "I'm babysitting, and the kid decided to dye her hair. I was trying to get the color out."

"Hey, no need to explain. I used to get into all sorts of scrapes when I was a kid," he said, passing me the receipt.

"Yeah? Like dying your hair blue?"

"Green." He chuckled and pulled at his collar. "Back then I idolized Oscar the Grouch and, hey it was picture day. What better way to start the school year, right? I even wore a matching t-shirt. And my lucky socks."

Okay, that made me laugh. "Did the socks work? What did your parents do?"

"I think my mom's hands looked like yours for a few days, but it didn't work. I have the picture on the wall to prove it. Never doubt the power of lucky socks."

I took a bite of the cookie and immediately made a noise of appreciation.

"You like it?" The corner of his lip went up again.

"You are a great baker," I said.

I swear pink crept up into his cheeks. "Aw, thanks. So, you new in town?" His voice had a melodious charm to it. His back was to me as he pulled out a tray of sugar cookies and set them on the counter. A moment later, he piped icing on them.

I nodded. "Yeah, sure am. And I'm about to go to my first job interview. Holy mother crackers, I'm nervous."

His eyebrow quirked as he glanced at me. "That's a funny saying. I used to know someone who said that. Years ago." He stretched his neck and adjusted his collar.

"Really? I learned it from my mom."

"Where are you from?"

"Charlotte. You been there?"

"Yeah, of course. It's only a little over an hour away. It must be a more common saying than I realized. Now where is this job interview at?"

I pointed in a general direction behind me. "Over at the second-hand store. Do you know the place?"

"Oh, the Sullivan sisters. Well, you're in for an adventure."

I stopped chewing. "What do you mean?"

He looked up and laughed. "Stop looking so worried. It will work out. They're nice, I promise. The kind who give out full-sized candy bars during trick-or-treating."

I took a sip and swallowed. "Sounds like you've been here a while. Do you know everyone?"

"Yeah, I grew up around here. My pop used to string electrical wires around this town before he retired. Probably worked on everyone of these poles."

"Wow." I nodded, my mind spinning on wondering how well he knew the town's people. Did he know Sam from the Farm and Feed? Maybe he'd have a clue where the guy was.

"Do you know a guy named Sam? He works at the—"

"Farm and Feed. Sure. Great guy. My dad's friends with him. You know him?"

"He was supposed to drop off some hay yesterday at my place but he never showed up."

"That's weird. He's super dependable. Rock solid even."

"That's what they were saying at the feed store."

"Yeah, He's had kind of a sad life. Lost his girlfriend after high school. Murdered. Never got over it. Where did you say your farm was at?"

"I'm here with my friend Tilly Miller. She has a little place out on Burn road."

"Yeah. Sure. I hear she's renting the old Douglas Glass place." He turned his back to me and rummaged in a drawer. I saw his finger dig into his collar again. Was I imagining it or was his tone decidedly cooler?

"I'm not sure about that, but she is renting it. We have a big barn and a cow."

"And a lot of excitement yesterday." He faced me again, and I was surprised to see his eyebrows furrowed together. "Listen, I'm not one to butt in, but you be careful. That was the mayor's cousin they found out there."

Geez. That was the second time I was being warned. Why did I need to be so careful? His words made my stomach squeeze like it did when there was a hurricane warning. Only this time I wasn't sure how to run from this storm.

CHAPTER 9

Tom glanced at the front door and then leaned closer. His voice lowered like he was about to spill some governmental secrets. "Clint McDaniel was known to dabble in stuff, you know what I'm saying? Had an addiction problem. He left town for years, decades even, and just recently moved back. Supposedly he was trying to get back on his feet after a bunch of bad luck. Well, you're new here too. And suddenly he's using again? It don't look good for you."

"Are you saying you think he got drugs from me?"

"I'm saying what it looks like to the mayor. Listen, I got to be careful talking about this. The mayor owns my place, along with half the town." He leaned back and began furiously polishing the glass counter with a cloth. "Now drink your coffee and go break a leg. I've got to go check on something in the oven."

He disappeared into the back room. I took another sip and then set the cup in a plastic tub by the coffee station before hollering goodbye. Tom shouted goodbye from the back, but there was no denying he'd cooled considerably.

I headed out to the car with an uneasy feeling. Tom was an odd read, wasn't he? I thought about his strange mannerisms, like the dismissive way he talked about baking like it was no big deal. And the way he tugged at his collar again and again. He'd done it right after Clint had been brought up, hadn't he?

Back in my car, I glanced at my phone for the time. Just a few minutes left before the interview. I needed to regroup and get on my "professional" face.

I pulled down the visor, making my nice blue hands came into view. I decided to shrug it off. Blue hands or not, I'd win those sisters over with personality and skills. I practiced my eager, interested smile. Think good thoughts, make them love ya.

I backed the car out of the stall and headed for the In For A Penny thrift store. Traffic was kind of crazy. Finally, I found a spot across from the business and parked. After locking the car, I ran down to the corner where I had to wait at the crosswalk. I probably looked like I was playing whack-a-mole with the way I was pushing the pedestrian button.

The crosswalk flashed green, and I started across. From the corner of my eye, I noticed a man staring at me through his windshield. I lifted my chin and ignored him, my normal reaction at unwanted ogling.

As I crossed in front of his car, he unrolled the passenger window. "Denise?" he called. His voice squeezed out, sounding panicked. "Denise Smith?"

I glanced at him, surprised. Was he talking to me?

Behind him a horn honked, making me jump. The light had turned green. The man started to speak again when the blasting horn cut him off for a second time. I ran to the other side. When I looked back he had hit the gas and was tearing through the intersection.

I watched him leave awash in confusion. What was that all about? What a weird day.

Slightly frazzled, I continued down the street and then up the stairs of the thrift store. An alarm announced my entrance with bird tweets. I grinned. It was cute.

A woman looked up from the counter. She had short gray hair puffed in a bouffant-type style and wore cat-eye glasses. Spread out over the counter's glass surface were many pieces of what appeared to be a complex puzzle.

"Hi, there," she said. "Welcome to In For A Penny. Can I help you find something?"

"Hi." I smiled, remembering just in the nick of time to stuff my hands into my jacket pockets. "I'm here for an interview? This place is amazing!"

"Ohh! Pammy! Come here and see the new girl!" Her thin eyebrows lifted above her eyeglass frame as she studied me. I was impressed with the amount of mascara her eyelashes carried as they swept against the lens. "And what's your name?"

"Chelsea Lawson," I said, striding over. I held out my hand.

She stared at my blue fingers like I was offering her a pile of worms. Immediately, my hand squeezed into a fist to hide itself. "I'm sorry," I said. "Hair dye accident with a six-year-old. She did it, I was trying to clean it out."

"Oh, honey. Never you mind about that," she said with a playful wave of her hand. Her fingers were covered in rings encrusted with enough jewels they could have doubled as a disco ball. "I have a few grandchildren myself. What won't they come up with to get into trouble? Pammy!"

This time, Pammy appeared from the back room. She was lithe and tall like the other woman and wore cat-eye eyeglasses as well. The main difference between the two women was the hair color. Both coiffures were in the same bouffant style, but Pammy's was a rich brunette.

"Oh! You must be Chelsea!" she said, walking over quickly, her legs sheathed in skinny jeans. "I'm Pam. I see you've met my sister, Polly. How do you do?" She grasped my hand and shook it enthusiastically with nary a glance at my Smurf-colored fingers.

"I'm good. Excited to be here!" I answered, feeling slightly breathless.

"Let me just show you around. You know, we were so impressed with your resume. You used to work with accounting?"

"Yes, for several years." I noticed she seemed wrapped in an odd scent, almost chemical of nature. I secretly sniffed, trying to place it.

"And why did you leave?" she asked.

"A friend needed me out here."

"Oh, that's nice. And do you like it in our little town of Cedar Falls? Isn't it amazing!"

I nodded again, trying not to think too deeply about the dead guy, the cow that liked to tap-dance on my shin, and the blue-haired child.

"I called your employer and they were most pleased with you and seemed dreadfully upset that you weren't returning." Pam smiled again. Her lipstick was the exact color I used to wear in high school. The name was candy-apple red. "Well over here is our consignment corner." She gestured to several bookshelves set up as space dividers. In each space was a decorated nook and filled with what appeared to be different antiques. Each nook had its own theme.

"We have clothing this way." She walked with quick steps, making me feel like I was scampering to keep up. "And down here is our housewares department."

Shelf after shelf was lined with plates, cups, pans, and tea kettles.

"Down here are our linens." A wooden dowel rack held a creamy avalanche of lace tablecloths. More shelves were filled with flannel sheet sets. Still another had towels.

"We have two industrial washing machines in the back. Everything goes in there first. If it can't be cleaned, it doesn't come in. No exceptions," Pam said. "I'm not risking even one critter coming in here, let alone go home with any of my dear customers. I have a reputation to uphold!" She reached for a towel to refold it.

"Got it." This was the most unusual job interview I'd ever had.

It was about to get stranger. "So, tell me. What's something you're afraid of?"

Her question shot a spike of adrenaline through me. I swallowed as my nightmare came to mind. Green grass. Strawberries. Red splotches.

Clearing my throat, I came up with a random fear. "Heights. I hate them."

"Ahh." She nodded sagely. "Well, in my long years I've learned that fear is just an emotion. You've got to squash that sucker every time it comes along and move on." She shook out another towel. "So, your application said you're free most days?"

"Yeah, I am. Except for this week. The little girl's mother is out of town so I need to be home when she gets out of school."

"Oh, of course. Well, very rarely will it be just you. Polly and I practically live here. Polly's always working on her puzzles, you see. And I have to tend the refurbs." She leaned in close. "I stain and repurpose them."

Ah! That explained the chemical smell. "Sounds great."

By now we'd made it around the interior and were back at the front desk. Pam grabbed my hand then and leaned back to study me. I had to resist an automatic reaction to pull away. Her head tipped, and she stared into my eyes. Finally, she nodded and released me. "I have a good feeling about you, Miss Chelsea. Can you start tomorrow?"

"Absolutely, after I get Emma off to school, I'll be here. Thank you."

"Wonderful. And just in time too. Tomorrow is doughnut day. Now I need to get back to my project!" With a small wave, she strode off to finally disappear into the back room.

Polly waved a puzzle piece at me. "See you tomorrow! Be here early or all the jelly-filled will be gone. Pammy's known for laying claim to them."

I thanked her and headed back outside amidst the bird chirps of the door alarm. I was happy, after all this seemed like a great job with good people. But niggling in the back of my mind was voice of the man who called me Denise earlier. The more time I spent here, the more of the town's strange quirks popped up. And my inside voice was warning me that things might not be exactly as they appeared.

CHAPTER 10

I was on a natural high from landing my job interview. Unfortunately, as Mark Twain once said so well, "To get the full value of joy you must have someone to divide it with." I glanced at the phone and tried to calculate the time difference before tossing math out the window. I called Mom with my fingers crossed that the signal was good, and she'd be able to pick up. After putting it on speaker, I drove out onto the road.

"Hi, sweetie!" Mom answered, making me smile.

"Hi, Mom! How is it going? Did I wake you?"

"No. We are—" The phone line crackled, and I cringed. We had a bad connection again. "Making good progress," she finished.

"I'm so proud of you! Guess what! I just got the job!"

"Oh, congratulations! I knew you would. And where is it again?"

I filled her in with all the details about In For A Penny thrift store. She did the appropriate amount of oohing and ahhing, making me smile.

"So." Her voice got business-like, indicating she was about to change the subject. "While I have you, what are we doing for Thanksgiving? I'll be home then. Are you driving back?"

I hadn't thought of that far ahead, to be honest. "Of course. Or you could come out here. What do you think about that?"

"That could work. You think Tilly would mind?"

I pulled a face as I realized I hadn't exactly cleared it with Tilly. Ah well. If it wasn't, then Mom and I would find a restaurant or something. Besides, I was fairly certain Tilly wouldn't care. "Of course not! And you could finally meet Emma."

Mom laughed. "The little six-year-old firecracker. Probably just like her mom used to be."

"That's right! And she lives up to her name, let me tell you."

She said she'd give it some thought as I pulled into the driveway. From where I sat, I could see Rosy out in the field. The cow saw me too and raised her head to moo in acknowledgment.

"Well, I'm home now and have to get ready for that firecracker," I said, reluctantly.

"Okay, sweetie. I'll talk to you soon."

I got out and waved at the cow. "Hi, Rosy! Are you going to come into the barn tonight like a good girl?"

Just then, a fierce squawking rocketed from the front of the house. I spun around, my blue hands held out in defense. Flying at me like a torpedo was a white-feathered mass of anger.

It took me a second to realize it was either a goose or a swan. And to say it did not look very happy was the understatement of the year.

The screeching bird raced toward me faster than I could think. What do I do? Where do I go? I darted to the other side of the car. The bird would not let up on the noise. I tried to keep the car between me and the bird. Finally, I had a chance to run to the porch. I scrambled for my keys while the bird dashed up the stairs after me.

"Go away!" I squeaked, snatching a cushion off the rocker to hold out like a shield.

The bird seemed satisfied that it had chased me up the stairs. With another harsh screech, it toddled off, head held high.

Dumbfounded. I watched it go in the direction of the field. I'd never seen it before. It wasn't Tilly's. Where the heck had that thing even come from?

Hands shaking, I managed to unlock the door. I'd hardly passed over the threshold when Jasper leaped out of nowhere, driving his paws straight into my mid-section. All the air knocked out of me, and I slithered to the floor, gasping, while the dog licked my face, my ear, and my hair.

Slowly, breath refilled my lungs. Jasper was extremely concerned and pawed me, maybe to get me to roll over or something. I'm not sure but his nails were sharp. I reached out, and he snuffled my hand. Still gasping, I stroked his ears. How could I be mad? He was giving me a whole Miller family welcome home.

Sore and feeling beat to a pulp, I struggled to sit up. I wasn't quite ready to stand yet, so I scooted over to the wall and leaned against it. Jasper barked and pranced before me, clearly entranced with the new game we were playing.

"Good boy. Go get your bone," I whispered. He wasn't distracted.

But I was. Something silver was under the foyer buffet. I reached for it, straining. My fingertips grazed it then pushed it in deeper. Finally, I was able to snag it out.

I sat up and held the item in my hand. It was the hook thing Emma had found. Maybe Jasper had knocked into it in his rush to get to me.

I dragged my purse closer. After scrambling for a moment, I retrieved my phone and texted Tilly. —**Hey, everything is okay here. Have time to talk?**

She typed back —**In just a minute**

I slowly rose to my feet and walked into the kitchen. There, the mess from the morning greeted me, crumbs and all. Exhaustion lay across my shoulders, and I heaved a big breath. Then, I got to work, first sweeping off the counter, putting the toaster away, throwing the blue-dyed towels into the washing machine and then locating the laundry soap. I was filling the dispenser when the phone rang.

"Chelz, is everything okay?" Tilly blurted out.

Text reassurance was nothing for a mom, I found. I wasn't eager to tell her what her daughter's hair looked like.

"Everything is going great. Emma is at school. Animals are all doing well. And Jasper really is a loving dog."

Her soft laughter carried through the speaker. "He sure is. I'm so glad it all went well. I didn't realize how sad I would be to not be there for Emma's first day of school."

I winced, as I was reminded how hard this must be for Tilly to be so far away. "She was excited." I glanced at the hook thing on the table. "She found something interesting yesterday."

"Oh, dear. That doesn't sound good. What is it?"

"I'm not sure. Can I send you a picture?"

"Yeah, go ahead."

I lined up in the phone's frame, snapped, and then hit send.

Her response was immediate. "I'm not sure. It could be the handle to the latch at the back gate. Sometimes they come that way when they drop off the hay.

Well, that's weird. That meant that it was possible that Sam, the Farm and Feed guy, might have shown up after all. Did he see all the crazy stuff and just take off? But why wouldn't he have left the hay?

Another thought hit me, this one more sinister. Did the murderer kidnap Sam?

"Shoot, I have to go. Anything more about Clint McDaniel?" I could hear voices in the background calling to Tilly.

"The police are doing drive-bys but they think it was specific to Clint. Otherwise, I haven't heard anything new."

"Okay. Make sure you lock up at night. Jasper will let you know if anyone comes to the door. Give Emma a kiss for me. I'll call her later."

"I'll let her know. And don't worry, I've got this."

"I know you do. Seriously, things are going so well here. I could never have done it without you. Honestly, I can never repay you."

"Repay me by getting nice and rich and famous."

She laughed, and we hung up. I turned to stare at the dog. "Now what?"

He tipped his head, ear perked.

"I guess you need to go outside and go potty—hmm?"

That must have been a yes, because, toe nails scrabbling, he skidded toward the front door. I ran for his leash so I could attach him to the outside lead.

It was then I spotted his food bowl which startled me because it was empty. Was that normal? Tilly had said he was to get just two scoops, but I didn't think that was enough. That must have been why the poor thing was so excited to see me. He was hungry. Maybe another half a scoop wouldn't hurt.

Jasper ran back in when he heard the kibble hit his bowl. I was horrified by the way he wolfed it up, like his mouth had turned into a vacuum cleaner. That couldn't be good for him.

"You need to chew that stuff or you're going to end up with a belly ache," I said as I snapped the leash into place.

He belched a big doggy burp into my face.

"Pee-ew!" I announced, and he did his best grin with his eyes squished and tongue lolling out. "Come on. Let's go."

I led him outside to the lead when he lunged forward barking. He nearly tore the leash out of my hands.

"What is it, buddy?" I asked, looking in the direction of his frantic barking.

It was then that I saw Rosy happily trotting down the driveway, leaving little clots of dust in the air.

My mouth dropped open. As if all the *Nos* in the world wrestled out of me, I punched out, "No! Rosy! Come back!"

Jasper took that as permission to lunge even harder, this time dragging me. I furiously looked for the lead's latch and managed to attach it, and then ran desperately after the cow.

CHAPTER 11

Panic made my feet move faster than they ever had before. How was I going to get that cow? The very cow that never listened to me to begin with?

"Rosy! Come here, girl!" I screeched and galloped after her.

I swear that tricky Holstein sped up. Her hooves clacked against the hard dirt road and her tail twitched.

"Rosy!" I yelled. Pain bloomed in my side. I clutched my stomach as I was forced to walk. I tried to keep my eye on her. Luckily, the road was as straight as a pin.

A horrible vision filled my head of her heading determinedly all the way down the road which emptied straight into main street. I could just picture cars veering and smashing into one another, and I nearly fainted with the instant panic. I started to jog again. I like cows. I like cows. I like cows.

"Rosy, come here, sweet girl!" I screamed again. My inner voice helpfully reminded me that this was not a dog I was chasing here.

Maybe she likes being called sweet girl, I argued back. Exhaustion can do that to a person. Make them argue with themselves.

The cow slowed for a moment, and one ear twitched back in my direction. Hope exploded in my chest. I put extra fire into my steps, my feet eating up the distance between us.

Unfortunately, I was still about thirty feet away when she started trotting again.

Hope drained out of me. I stopped and watched her go, leaning my hands on my knees and gasping for air. My lungs were on fire. Tears burned my eyes.

You can't give up. Stick with her. You'll figure it out as you go.

I straightened my back as my muscles blazed with protestation. Rosy was under my watch. I wasn't going to let her go. Slowly, I began walking again.

My mouth was as dry as carpet from all my panting, and sweat ran down my back. My hair felt like a dusty mop. I glanced at my watch, mentally kicking myself for forgetting my phone. Emma would be home in two hours.

I looked back at the road, and a gasp ripped out of me.

The cow had vanished.

As in gone, gone. No puff of dust from clattering hooves,

no black-and-white Oreo body joggling ahead. Stiffly, I trotted down the road to where I last saw her.

There was a driveway that had been hidden by the tall wild grass. I glanced down it to see Rosy already at the other end and about to disappear around the side of a house.

"Rosy!" I yelled. I needed to go after her but I was a little worried. Out here, people had dogs to protect their property. And guns. But Tilly had mentioned the neighbors were nice. I only hoped that was true.

No time to worry about it now. I had to get that cow. I walked down the driveway. By the time I reached the house— a lovely two-story white building with blue shutters just the shade of my fingers— the cow was out of sight again.

I slowed down and tried to decide if I should first knock on the door, or just run around the house and nab that cow— although with my luck risking running into a nudist autumn sunbather—when I heard singing, loud and warbling, coming from the left of the building. I walked over there and came upon an old greenhouse.

I tried to catch my breath and probably sounded like my lungs were bellows in an ancient iron factory. "H-hello!" I infused the best friendly tone as I could as I tried not to pass out.

"Hey, there," called a woman from inside. When she didn't come out, I stuck my head through the doorway. The woman was crouched over a planter with her hands deep in black dirt. Tiny plants in little egg cartons sat at her feet. There were bigger plants on the side wall, with the biggest ones in the very back.

"I'm not interested in any magazine subscriptions," she said, still not standing.

"What?"

"And I already support the schools."

"No, I—"

This time she did look up. Her cheeks were ruddy, and her gray frowsy hair was pulled back in a patterned yellow scarf. "I'm trying to tell you that I don't buy from solicitors. Sorry."

With her eyebrows lowered into a decidedly unfriendly expression, I wasn't sure how to tell her my cow was possibly knee-deep in her tulips, happily munching every flower head off.

I tried again. "Sorry to barge in like this. I'm the neighbor. Actually, I'm more house sitting. And the cow just escaped and has disappeared behind your house, and—"

"Oh, my stars, my prized Dwarf Crested Iris!" She sprung up with more energy than I thought one could at her age. I stepped back to avoid her dirty gloved hands as she flew past me. "Well, come on. We can't let her get them! She'll mow through them like she's a John Deere tractor."

She skirted through the yard and around the corner of the house. I jogged after her. What was with all this speed everyone had? By the time I reached her, she had the cow by the ear and was steering the animal back toward me.

The woman shook her head as I watched in astonishment. "Young lady, you need to shut that pie hole right quick. We have hornets around here. They're liable to make a nest. My goodness, you are new around here, aren't you? No, I'm not hurting her. I'm letting her know who's boss. By the way, my name's Sharon. Sharon Rabb." Her green rubber boots stepped firmly through the lawn.

The cow seemed to know who was boss, that's for sure. She followed obediently alongside the lady with nary a wayward hoof in sight.

When Sharon reached me, she motioned as if offering me the ear. I gingerly grabbed it between two fingers, wanting to whisper an apology to Rosy.

Her frown immediately came back. "No. Not so prissy-like. Oh, here, give it to me. I suppose I should see you home."

We walked down the driveway, with me following like a little duckling. At the road I hurried to catch up to walk by her side.

"So what happened at your place yesterday morning, anyway?" Sharon asked.

I swallowed, not at all sure of how many details the police had released. Finally, I decided to spill my guts. After all, she was the neighbor.

"We found a man in the barn yesterday morning. Unfortunately, he was dead." I glanced anxiously at her. I didn't want to be the one to give her the bad news.

"Oh, sure. Clint McDaniel. He died of an overdose, right?"

I narrowed my eyes. So she did know what had happened. She was just fishing for any details I might have to give. Well, maybe she had some information herself. I liked to fish as well. "Apparently, the toxic load was so much the medical examiner has ruled it a murder."

"My goodness, a murder in these parts." She let out a low whistle. "Clint McDaniel. I always knew he'd be up to no good. I tell you what. I'm not surprised at all."

We'd finally reached the driveway to Tilly's farm. It was about two seconds later when I started to scream.

CHAPTER 12

At least, I tried to scream. Instead, what came out was an unintelligible croak that probably had the nearby frogs feeling kinship.

"What the tarnation is wrong with you?" Sharon said with mild disapproval.

The words still wouldn't come, lodged behind a muzzle of horror. I pointed to my car.

On the hood, like the world's sprightliest mountain climber, was the billy goat. He bleated as though to celebrate his success and then leaned down to take a bite from my windshield wiper.

"Your goat's escaped as well?" All given in a monotone, I had no idea what Sharon was thinking.

I nodded mutely, about one second away from throwing in the towel.

"Well, don't you worry none. We'll fix their curve and get that fence secure in no time flat. Let's just get this runner here to her stable."

She walked to the barn while I tried to shoo the goat off the hood. After a few lazy blinks, he clattered down, his hooves leaving neat little dents on the hood.

In the meantime, Sharon reappeared, shaking a can of feed. The goat scampered in her direction at the sound of the rattle. We found the other goat and penned her as well.

Then Sharon and I walked over to the fence.

"Wow, that's a doozy. That cow must have been in a hurry to get out."

"I don't think Rosy has ever done something like this before."

"Cows, you never do know with them."

It was then I saw tire tracks. Odd ones, closer together than the width of a car tire, but meatier. The dirt was churned up where they had dug in.

"What's that do you think?" I pointed.

Sharon crouched down. "Looks to me to be a four-wheeler."

We both turned to stare in the direction the tracks came from. Now that I was standing in the line of sight, I could see a slight trail in the grass.

"Came from across your pasture," Sharon continued.

"I don't see how?"

"My guess is that your fence is down someplace else."

"Tilly told me we have a gate back there that leads to the barn."

"Well then it's open. Have you had a walk around the fence?"

I shook my head. No, despite how ordinary and boring the day had been so far, it hadn't crossed my mind to walk the many acres of the field. Sarcastic, even to myself. I took a deep breath, realizing that's just what I was about to do.

I glanced at my watch. "Emma's going to be home in forty-five minutes."

"That's enough time. Just put a little pepper in your step, and we've got this." She stalked off in her rubber boots at a furious speed. I shook my head. Country living got you in shape, I had to give it that.

Determined not to once again look like a duckling chasing after the momma duck, I hurried to match her pace.

We followed the fence through some beautiful country. Trees spread out before us in what appeared to be living ocean waves of glowing leaves. There were splotches of yellow, red, brown and green, like someone had shaken a paint brush across the scene.

"So, with everything that happened, how safe are you feeling around here?"

"I'm okay. The police are driving by, and I have Jasper."

Sharon sucked on her teeth. "When I was a young girl, we left our doors unlocked. Times have never been the same since the bank robbery."

"What was that?"

"Oh, about twenty years past. Town bank got robbed and the cashier was held at gun point to open the safe. She did and still got killed. Town's never been the same since then."

"Wow! Did they ever catch the robbers?"

She shook her head.

Right then I stepped into something soft. I stared at the ground in alarm, fearing the worst, but it turned out to be swampy mud from an underground spring. Sharon sloshed through it with nary a blink, while I picked my way around, probably appearing like I was trying to navigate through a pile of mouse-traps. I understood now why she wore rubber boots.

A couple of minutes later we found the second breach. The gate was open and had been pushed back against its hinges.

"Well, you're lucky that cow didn't escape out this way," Sharon noted. "Down there is a pond and Running Creek, and even further is a drop-off."

"I didn't realize there was a creek back here."

"Yeah, it connects to a river. My cousin runs boats up and down it for tourists. You ever want a trip, you tell him I sent you." She gave the gate an experimental tug. "Whoever came through was in a hurry. Bent the post."

I pushed on the post attached to the twisted hinge, trying to figure out what to do next.

"You keep that cow in her stall for a bit longer. I'll call Roy and have him stop by." Sharon nodded again.

"Who's Roy?" I asked.

"Oh, he's my handy man. He'll get this fixed, no worries."

"I don't have a lot of money," I admitted.

"That's his specialty, cheap fixes." She patted my arm. "Don't you worry none. From the looks of your hands, you've got enough to worry about."

I laughed and explained what happened. She grinned as well. "I've always liked that girl. Emma is a spit-fire." She tipped her head. "Where you from again?"

"Charlotte"

"Huh. Big city girl, huh? Never been up that way. You look like someone I used to know way back when. Well, we need to be getting back. I've got my own animals I need to round up." She tipped her head. "Speaking of animals, you haven't seen a gander around here recently?"

Memories of my flight around the car came to mind. "Oh, yeah! He chased me up the porch!"

She sighed, air hissing between her teeth. "That boy is my guard goose. But every now and then he wants to chase the ladies down at the pond back there. You weren't hurt none?"

I shook my head. "Scared me, though!"

"Just be glad he wasn't a turkey. A pack of those things can be worse than wild dogs."

I glanced at my watch. "Emma will be off soon. I better head back."

We trudged straight across the field this time. I did keep an eye out for any patties. I figured if I were to step in something soft again, I wouldn't be as lucky as last time.

"So, you said you knew Clint McDaniel?" I asked after a while. Time to cast my fishing line.

"Yeah. Funny thing, he's been out of town for a while. I'm surprised he's back."

"Oh, really?"

"He left for the big city years ago, to make his mark on society, I suppose. We were all young and dumb back then. Would you believe I won the title School Prankster?"

"You both went to school together?" Now I felt sad for her.

"Yeah, we sure did. Didn't like him then, and I can't say my opinion improved through the years. He was flashy, always tried to do things the easy way, and didn't mind dragging any naive chump along with him."

I made a face. "So, it sounds like he might have made a few enemies then?"

"He could charm a honeycomb off of a brown bear's hairy paw when he felt like it. But you couldn't trust him. As soon as he found someone better, he'd move on to the next."

"Do you think he got into drugs?" I asked.

"That's what I heard. Partied with the best of them."

By now we'd reached the front breach in the fence. Carefully, we picked over the wires. I reached back to help her, but she was already over it.

"Like I said, someone was in a rush to get out of here. You didn't hear it?"

I shook my head, slightly embarrassed.

"Hang on a second," I said, and jogged into the house. I grabbed the hook and brought it out. "What do you make of this?"

"Oh easy. It's what they use to pick alfalfa hay bales up with." She pointed to the hay that the Farm and Feed had brought in its emergency delivery. "The man probably dropped it delivering that."

I nodded. But I knew it had been here before the delivery. Back when the delivery guy had disappeared.

Sharon clucked for her goose, and he came waddling out at her voice. "What are you doing, George?" she scolded and picked him up. Shielding her eyes, she stared out at the barn. "Sure is a shame what happened. Hope it doesn't color your perception of our town none."

"I really like it," I reassured her.

"Me too, with the exception of our mayor. Honestly, I wouldn't be surprised if it was him who knocked his cousin off, truth be told."

CHAPTER 13

My mouth dropped. "The mayor?"

"He's got political aspirations. And that cousin of his was no good. Mayor McDaniel especially needs to watch his Ps and Qs because he has a real chance of losing the election this year. Laura Owens is running against him, and she's a smart cookie. She's got a rebuttal to every one of his arguments and can really shut his pie-hole." She shrugged. "In the end, I always suspected the mayor bribed Clint to go away all those years ago. Then Clint came back. Maybe the mayor thought of another way to handle it." She winked. "But you didn't hear that from me." She straightened and began walking briskly toward the road. "I'll have the handy man come out to repair the fence. Just a heads up. Roy's a bit rough around the edges, but he's one in a million. Now, let's go home, George."

The two of them had made it a few feet past the driveway when the school bus swayed down the road like a yellow hippopotamus. She waved at the driver as he passed her and then ducked her face at the rising dust.

I headed to the end of the driveway to wait for Emma.

The bus stopped with a squeak and a shudder that indicated worn-out struts. The doors opened and, amidst screams of goodbyes and laughter, Emma bounded out with blue hair cascading around her shoulders. Fantastic. So much for my bun idea to hide it.

Eyes wide, she streaked past me and toward the house in a whirl of wind and hair flying behind. "I've got to use the bathroom!"

I followed after her, reaching the porch as the bathroom door slammed shut.

Jasper barked to remind me he was still on his lead.

"Come here, boy." I got him unclipped and led him into the house.

All right, next get a snack for Emma. I opened the cupboards and searched through the shelves. Soon, cheese in a can and crackers on a plate joined a basket already filled with napkins on the kitchen table. I rummaged in the fridge and added a glass of milk, and a few slices of pepperoni to the plate. Jasper watched my every move, his eyebrows jumping up and down over each eye.

Now, where was she?

I headed down the hallway. The bathroom door was left

open with no Emma in sight. I traveled upstairs to her room but she wasn't there either.

"Jasper! Where's Emma?" I asked. The dog wagged his fringy tail like it was a flag and bounded back down the stairs. I followed the dog to find Emma sitting at the table with a box of crayons and a huge piece of orange construction paper. Geez, she could be quiet when she wanted to be.

"What a good dog." I scratched his ears to thank him for finding her.

Then I noticed the cat was curled up in the napkin basket. I scooped him out and set him onto the floor. He flounced away, greatly displeased with me.

"Hi, Emma. How was your day?"

"Good," she said. Her swinging legs thumped against the chair rails.

"Well, that's good. Do you like your snack?"

"Yeah," she said. She paused in her drawing to do one careful line of cheese on a cracker and popped the creation into her mouth.

"So, I see your hair is down. Did anyone say anything?"

"They thought it was cool," she said, simply.

"Were you able to get some lunch?"

She nodded and stood up, fishing the change out of her pocket and setting it on the table. A couple of the coins rolled toward the edge. I swatted them down before they fell off.

"Thanks, Emma! So do you have any homework tonight?"

She shook her head, her tongue poking out to the side as she drew.

"What are you drawing?" I tried again.

"I'm drawing a picture. It's my favorite person. Besides my momma, I mean." She looked at me and smiled.

Oh, my gosh. She meant me. My heart melted, and I wanted to grab her in a hug. But I knew she didn't like touching, so I leaned over her shoulder to see what it was.

Huh. If that was me I had short hair. And a mustache. "Who's that?"

"It's Mr. Frank. He's my teacher."

"Your teacher is your favorite person?"

She nodded and drew a flower next to him. And then another, along with a big smilie face.

"What's that?" I pointed to the face.

"That's Rosy. She's bringing him flowers."

Way to rub salt in the wound. "Are you sure she's not eating them, instead?" I grumbled. "Or maybe getting ready to give him a kick?"

Jasper jumped up on the couch and began barking. I glanced out the window in time to see a white truck pull into the driveway. It was lifted with chrome accents, and I could tell the guy was having fun, like pedal-to-the-metal kind of fun. He slowed at the driveway and entered respectfully. On the side of his truck was a decal that said, "The Caretaker. How may I care for you?"

I walked to the porch as the truck jolted to a stop. A thin older man jumped out. He had dark hair, a mustache, and sparkling eyes. "Well, hello there! My name's Roy. Sharon told me to you needed some help."

"I so appreciate you coming out so fast." I skipped down the steps and showed him the fence.

He gave a low whistle and stooped to pick up a broken post. "Okay. It's been crazy around here lately for you, hasn't it? Sharon said a regular disaster zone."

I lifted my eyebrows at the description, but what could I say? "It's been pretty bizarre. Did you know the guy that died?"

His lips thinned and disappeared under the mustache. "Can't say it was my pleasure. But I knew people who knew him."

"And...?"

"Let's just say I don't exactly hang with that crowd. Good way to end up on the wrong side of a prison door."

"Wow, so he was some type of criminal, huh?"

"Some type of something, anyway. I don't get too close to find out. After all, if something happened to me, who would take care of my dog?"

As if the animal had heard his owner, a black-and-white face poked out the driver's window.

"Oh, my gosh! He's adorable!"

"Thanks! Found him running along the highway one day. Poor bugger got dropped off by some scumbag."

"Aww." Pain squeezed my heart. "I'm so glad you found him."

"Hard to believe people are really that cold-hearted. But there are some real monsters out there. You can take that to the bank."

He headed back to his truck and pulled out a post hole digger. "All right, I'm going to get started. Sharon said there was also a post broken at the gate?"

"Yes, over there on the other side. Hang on a sec. Let me go check on Emma." I ran inside to find her still drawing. When I returned, he'd already cut the old post free from the wire and had restrung the fence.

"Wow! You're fast."

"Been stringing fence most of my life." He gave the new post a final pat. "Okay, I'll be back in a few." He opened the truck door for his dog and whistled. As he tromped through the field, I could swear I heard him singing. The dog leaped at his feet as if joining the joy.

He might say there were monsters out there, but I was finding more and more hidden gems the longer I lived.

CHAPTER 14

That morning, I had the nightmare again. I woke up sweating and heaving as if I'd just run a marathon. Strawberries and grass, red smears. Sign posts. Tears rolled from my eyes, and I squeezed them tight, trying to make the images disappear.

I have the right to live. I have the right to live. I have the right to live.

I rolled over and grabbed my wallet to look at the photo. Mom was so beautiful. And there I was in that funny little dress, always looking at my profile in the mirror.

After a moment the dream eased away, allowing reality to fit back into a nice safe shape. The cow mooed, the dog barked, and from some place in the house, a door slammed. Time to start the day.

But I needed a bit more coddling. I dug around my

suitcase that I'd still not completely unpacked until I found my pink fuzzy socks. Soft like duckling down, they were practically like slippers, and I loved them.

Then life became like an assembly line. Breakfast for the kid, the dog and cat, the cow, the goats, and the bunnies. Back inside to make sure Emma was dressed, teeth brushed, dog on the lead, books packed and kid being walked to the end of the driveway. I was starting to feel like a pro.

"You have your lunch money?" I asked as we waited for the bus.

"Uh huh. I get chocolate milk today." Her gapped smile made me grin too.

"Oooh, I'm jealous," I said, reaching out to tousle her hair.

She didn't let me. Instead, she skipped ahead, arms out, and was walked along Roy's tire track like it was an imaginary tightrope.

The bus rolled down the road in all its mustard yellow glory. Emma jumped up and down and then twirled in a circle on her toe. As it approached, I got a firm grip on the strap of her backpack to hold her back, and we waited less than patiently for the bus to squeal to a stop.

The door opened, and I sent her off again to the hoard of screaming zoo animals otherwise known as elementary school-age kids.

Through the windows I could see her little brown pigtails as she bounced down the aisle and into the seat with her friend. Fortunately, it turned out that the eight hair washes was really one long wash with a capful of diluted vinegar. They both turned to look at me and wave like they were in a parade. I waved back, and the bus drove off.

After a quick shower, and another scoop of food for poor Jasper who looked at me so pitifully, I climbed into the car to head to work. As I started the engine, I stared at the hoof prints all over the windshield. Pressing my lips together, I pressed the windshield wiper fluid switch. Liquid sprayed the glass, and the wipers did their best to clear it. Unfortunately, the rubber part of the wipers was notched with little goat teeth marks.

Rolling my eyes, I backed out of the driveway. Just as soon as I hit the road, I was serenaded with a weird rattle coming from the engine compartment. Not a normal weird noise, one that sounded like a very important piece was about to fall out.

Fantastic. I flipped the music volume higher to drown it out.

As I drove, I started to think about the mayor. Had Sharon actually inferred that he could be responsible for his cousin Clint's murder? She had. And no amount of fancy speech, winking eyes, or shrugging shoulders of innocence could take that away.

Tom from Sweet Buns Bakery sure clammed up when he realized Clint had died at my house. He said he had to be careful. That made the mayor sound vindictive. I wondered if Mayor McDaniel knew about me?

The thought chilled me more then when I had to go into the deep freezer when I worked as a teen at the grocery store.

I was lucky enough to find a spot to park near the front

of In For A Penny. I couldn't forget the last time I'd been here, when that creepy guy yelled that woman's name at me. I glanced around a bit like I thought he could still be lurking, before hurrying out of my car and up to the door. Just before I went in, I turned to press the lock on the car fob.

The store was as bright and cheery as yesterday. There was a huge box of doughnuts on the counter and Polly was working on a puzzle that seemed to be about fifty percent finished.

"Why hello, you!" Polly called after snapping in a piece. "Want a doughnut?"

"Hi!" I said, shrugging off my coat. "Maybe in a little bit. Where can I put this?"

"Suit yourself. Just put it back there." She indicated with a lifting of her elbow to the back room.

I headed back there where I was greeted with a table and a wall of coat hooks. I hung up my jacket and took a quick peek of myself in the antique wall mirror. I had to give myself a thumbs up. Even with my crooked eyetooth, I was looking pretty descent.

"Hello, dear, how are you?" asked Pam.

I spun around, surprised at how she'd snuck up on me.

Her tone was weird, like something was wrong. The expression she gave me mimicked the mood with a pair of lowered, concerned eyebrows.

"I'm fine," I said, with a smile, feeling decidedly unsure. "You been busy?"

"Only baking. We make supper once a week for someone in our church, depending on who is in need."

"Oh, that's nice."

She shook her head and stirred her tea. "What's not so nice is how gossip gets around." Here she shot me another look.

"Oh," I said, "You must mean Clint."

"Yes dear, only you need to be a bit more careful."

"What do you mean?"

"The mayor is telling everyone it was a heart attack while unloading your hay."

"Hay? He didn't unload any hay at my place."

Two things happened simultaneously. The first was a flush of indignation that rolled over my face. The second were prickles rising on the back of my neck. People were talking about me. And not in a good way.

Years of being gossiped about, complete with fingers pointing, people bending their heads to whisper, and shocked gazes coupled with smothering hugs squeezed my heart tight. Not again. This couldn't be happening again. I'd fought for anonymity for years. I coveted it.

Strawberries and green grass. I'd do anything to protect it.

"Okay, I'll be careful," I whispered. I glanced at the exit, wanting to run away.

"I'm not trying to worry you, dear, but you need to be. That's the mayor's cousin. He doesn't take lightly to any offense against his family."

"What's the offense? I'm not sure I understand?"

She leaned close to whisper and brought that strange chemical odor that was mixed with the scent of spaghetti. "They say you're telling people it was drugs."

People? What people? Instead of defending myself, I nodded, needing to end the conversation. "I'm not talking to anyone about him. I'll make sure it stays that way."

She handed me a dust rag and sent me out to check the shelves. I walked back to the corner she indicated, a Lot eight, and started dusting. It was an antique toy booth. I could feel tears well in my eyes as I straightened the old doll dresses and dusted around miniature iron cookstoves. But when I came to the toy airplane, I lost it. This toy was hitting too close to home, to my nightmare. I had to call Mom.

I found Polly at the counter and asked for a quick bathroom break.

"Of course." She eyed me shrewdly. "Are you okay?"

I nodded, but my sniffle gave me away. At her permission, I ran for the back room where the bathroom was hidden behind a load of boxes and old furniture left to be sorted.

Fingers crossed and a lump in my throat, I dialed. I almost broke with relief when the call went through.

"Hi, Mom," I said in a hushed tone.

She didn't beat around the bush. "Chelsea, I'm on my way out to the job site. Are you okay? You're worrying me."

"Not so great right now." I squeezed my eyes tight. I couldn't tell her. I had to be strong.

But I so desperately wanted to release the pain. The memories.

What if it was my fault?

That tiny guilty fear.

And the second fear, its brother... why was I saved?

They were questions that haunted me for months after the incident. In fact, every night of my eighth year I went to bed convinced that I was going to die.

Until my appendix surgery, when I woke up out of anesthesia, my head foggy and my mouth tasting like a chemical wasteland. I realized then I had to live. And I had to live a life worthy of all the huge loss in my past.

Part of being worthy was not burdening my mom again.

"What's the matter, Chelsea?" Mom asked again softly. I realized she was stopping everything to give me time. I could hear the compassion in her voice, wrapped in memories of freshly baked cookies, clean sheets and a cold wash cloth on my forehead while she dragged the little TV into my room when I was sick.

She was the best. She'd had to raise me all alone. She was the epitome of a mom.

I swallowed again and then grabbed a towel to wipe under my eyes. "It's just this new job. So many things. It gets overwhelming."

There was a silence. One beat. Two. Did she believe me? Was she remembering the past incident too?

When she responded her voice was like a professional poker player. She never exposed what she was thinking. "Try to get to bed earlier tonight. You're going to be okay. Are you eating? I had a care package sent to you from our favorite online store. It should be arriving today. I wanted to celebrate your new job. I'm proud of you."

I chucked the towel as I stared at my puffy-eyed reflection in the mirror. "Thanks, Mom. I just needed to hear that."

And then she slipped. "You are a survivor, Chelsea. Remember that."

My bottom lip trembled. I pressed it tight. Finally, I nodded and gulped out, "Mom. You are the best."

"Okay, sweetie. I love you. I need to let you know if you can't reach me, don't worry. Reception is getting even more sketchy over here with the storm that's coming. I promise I'll stay safe. And you stay safe as well."

"I will. I love you, too." I hung up and splashed cold water on my face. I patted my cheeks dry and then pointed fiercely to my reflection. "You *are* a survivor. Never forget that."

Feeling a bit heavy and emotionally wobbly, I headed back to my dusting job. The rest of the day passed weirdly. There was one point that I could have sworn I saw two customers give me a weird stare and ask Polly who I was. After she told them I was Chelsea the new employee, they sent me furtive glances and turned their backs to me while whispering.

How had this rumor started with Clint's death being pinned on me? The only person I'd spoken about the overdose with was Sharon. Had she told everyone?

I tried to pretend I wasn't feeling miserable as I finished my shift. Finally it was time to clock out and go meet Emma's bus.

Back at the car, the darn engine did its crazy new shake,

rattle, and roll so I blasted the music again to cover the noise. I'd have to figure out what was wrong at some point, but today was not that day.

As I pulled into the driveway, the mailman could be seen coming down the road. Mom said the package should be here, so this was perfect timing. I slammed the door and walked out to the mailbox.

I realized then that we hadn't had any mail yesterday. That was odd. I'd personally never had a day go by before without some type of junk mail.

The mailman left Sharon's mailbox and approached ours. I was surprised to see how fast he was coming. His car dragged a plume of dust, and he didn't appear to be slowing down any. Maybe he didn't see me? I stepped out from behind the mail box to be sure I was seen.

The mail truck flew by me without him giving me the slightest glance. I watched him leave, mouth hanging. Not only was there no care package, but there was no mail. Again? Well, that's just great. I guess I'd have to stop by the post office tomorrow. Maybe the package was too big.

Frustrated, I stomped toward the house. I let out Jasper, who proceeded to jump on me, pushing me back into the wall. I needed to figure this dog out or he was going to knock me over in his eagerness to greet me. As he licked my hands I realized that right now his love was exactly what I needed. I waited until he calmed down a bit and then pulled him into a bear hug and buried my face into his fur.

His scent was warm and clean, and he squirmed around

until he could fawn over my face. Too late, I realized he was cleaning my tears. He breathed a hot doggy smile on me, and I stroked his neck.

"I love you too, Jasper. You ready to go outside?"

I grabbed him by the collar and got him out to his lead, and then refilled his water bowl. His food bowl was empty again. Concerned, I gave him another scoop. Then, I started dinner and prepared Emma's snack.

A short while later, the bus pulled up. Emma jumped off the bus while I watched from the front door. She bounded into the house and into the bathroom, while I released an eager Jasper from the lead to go greet his girl.

"Hi, Emma!" I called as I came inside and shut the front door.

"Hullo!" She swept past with lightning energy and into the kitchen, where she inhaled her crackers and milk and was already running toward her room before I had a chance to remove all her books from her backpack.

"Did you have a good day at school?" I called after her.

"Uh huh!" she hollered.

A moment later, her door slammed. I would have pursued more of a conversation with her but I'd come across an envelope in her backpack that was addressed to Chelsea Lawson.

I pulled it out, very confused. Why would she have an envelope with my name on it? Carefully, I slid my finger under the seal and opened it, then pulled out the folded note paper.

At the top was the school's heading. It was from her teacher, and in simple script it said.

Ms. Lawson, I understand you are watching Emma Miller for the week. We have a little issue I need to go over with you. Can you meet me in the classroom during lunchtime tomorrow?

After that was his name, Jason Frank, and the room number.

I stared at it, suddenly very concerned at what this might bring.

Just then Rosy mooed and Jasper barked. I didn't need any more signs to prove that I was definitely in over my head.

CHAPTER 15

A s I stared at the letter, I realized that Emma had
been in her room for a while. Quiet. Concern
prompted me to hurry and check on her.

I walked down the hall where I heard a little voice
chiming in adamantly, "Jimmy, you better let that go. We don't
bite heads. Or beds."

What kind of game was she playing? I tapped on the door
and then cracked it open to peek inside. "Emma, are you
okay?"

She looked up from where she sat in front of a dollhouse.
"Oh, hi, Chelsea."

I felt better just seeing her. She wasn't dyeing something
blue or creating some mastermind scheme to conquer the
world. "What are you doing? Playing with your dollhouse?"

"Uh huh," she answered and held out a little doll to show me. "Me and Jimmy and Rose."

"Ah, how fun. Is that Rose?"

She rolled her eyes like I'd just asked if the sky was pink. "No."

"Uhh, Jimmy?" I chucked out.

"This is the dad," she corrected. "And that's the mom." She reached in and pulled out another doll.

Not Jimmy or Rose. Okay, maybe she had a few more invisible friends? Were these Freckles's friends? Should I continue to ask questions or was that discouraging creativity? I truly didn't get this parent gig. I couldn't believe Tilly said this would be easy.

I tentatively tried again. "Can Jimmy see me?"

She shook her head in the negative. I honestly was stumped. "Where is he?" I finally asked.

"In there." Her tiny finger pointed into the dollhouse.

I entered the room, navigating around a set of blocks and a stack of books, and then leaned down to peer inside.

Whiskers and beady eyes stared back at me. I screamed and stumbled back.

"What are you doing? Don't scare him." She reached inside and stroked the animal.

I peeked in again. It was a rabbit. Two rabbits, to be exact. They sat in the dollhouse living room, ears straight up, noses wiggling a mile a minute. While I watched, one of the bunnies picked up a chair and started nibbling on it.

"Uh, how long have they been here?" I asked as my heart finally settled back into a normal rhythm.

"All day. I brought them in this morning. I thought they might be bored in their cage."

One bunny finished its nibbling on the little chair. Now that it had my attention, I saw the chair was already missing three legs. "Come on, let's bring the bunnies back to their cage. They look like they might be tired."

I scooped up one heavy bunny, supporting his hind legs, while Emma did the same to the other one. We carried them to the barn and put them in their cage.

While out there, I saw that Rosy had returned to her stall. Thank goodness. I used the rake trick to shut the cow's gate when I heard a weird noise. It was an animal, but one that was low and stressed. It was then I noticed one of the goats hadn't gotten up from where it had been laying this morning.

"That's Daisy," Emma said as she fed her bunnies.

Immediately, I knew something was wrong. I fished my phone from my pocket and called the emergency vet's number that Tilly had left for me.

"Hello?" A deep masculine voice answered.

"Hi, I'm here at Tilly Miller's farm. I know nothing about animals, but one of the goats hasn't gotten up from this morning."

There was no hesitation. "I'll be right out."

He hung up before I gave him my address. He must know this place.

I sent Emma to the house to take a shower while I waited

for the vet. I had no idea what to do as I hovered around the stall door, anxiously peering in. Would I disturb the poor animal even more if I went inside?

I spotted a small butter container on the shelf and filled it with water, then brought it in to Daisy.

The goat's eyes were closed, and it was breathing slowly. I suddenly felt mortifyingly under qualified to take care of a house plant, let alone anything with a heartbeat. If anything happened to this animal under my watch, I'd be crushed. Hurry, vet! Hurry!

Softly, I stroked her forehead. "You're going to be okay. I'm here."

After briefly opening her eyes, Daisy ignored the water. I sat quietly to keep her company. Even Rosy seemed to realize something was wrong. She didn't make much noise other than to rustle in her stall.

A while later, I finally heard the crunching of tires down the driveway. There was a car door slamming and then footsteps. I was about to leave my patient to let him know where I was but I could hear footsteps approaching. He must have assumed I was in the barn.

"Hello?" the man called when entering.

"Back here!"

He approached me, carrying a bag. "Hi, there," he said as he pushed up his flannel shirtsleeve and opened the stall door.

"I'm so glad you're here! This is Daisy."

He squatted down next to the goat. First he checked her gums and then her eyes. "How long has she been like this?"

"I noticed she seemed mellow this morning when I opened the gate. But I thought maybe she'd just woken up." I cringed. "I'm sorry I'm so dumb. I'm new to animals."

"You did the right thing to call me."

Gently, he checked the animal over. "She's pregnant?"

I swallowed and stared. "I don't know. Is she?"

"Yup. Must be a big baby because he's stuck."

My whole world shifted right then. I felt terrible. I wished the ground would open and swallow me up. I felt like a failure.

"If you don't have experience with animals then you couldn't have known," he said, opening up his bag. He pulled on a pair of gloves that went clear to his elbows and got out some cleanser. He squirted a few pumps and then went to check the animal.

The poor goat let out a gust of air.

"Little tangle in here, but the baby is fine."

"How can you tell?"

"Little stinker tried to nip my fingers," he said with a grin. "Might have to call this one Jaws. And the other one kicked at me. He must be Kangaroo Jack."

The vet was teasing, but I was still shocked. "There are two?" I asked.

"Usually it's fine, but in this case the twins were trying to race each other out first. Always causes some trouble." His face scrunched, and he adjusted his arm. "You go back in there. You'll get your turn in a minute. Now you, come here, little guy. Let's get this show on the road. Your caretaker is worried." His piercing blue eyes caught me then. "And what was your name again?"

"Chelsea."

"Chelsea, hmmm. When I was a kid I had a crush on a rock star named Chelsea." He hummed a few bars, making me smile. He pushed around a bit more. "My name's AJ." Then he addressed the goat again. "All right, love, it's all situated. Why don't you give a push?"

She seemed to know things were better because she grunted.

"That's right, keep her coming." The vet guided a tiny hoof out. The second one followed.

The goat strained some more and out shot a wet baby goat into the vet's arms.

"Oh, good job, momma!" I said, patting her neck before bending down to give her a kiss. I have to admit, I teared up a bit.

"You have a towel?" AJ asked.

I had no idea if we did so he snatched up a handful of straw and began massaging the baby animal. Momma goat turned to sniff the baby. I swear she gave a chuckle in pleasure.

Moments later, she strained again.

"Chelsea?" A little voice called urgently.

I looked up, happy as anything. "Look, Emma! Our goat had a baby!"

Emma licked her bottom lip. "Chelsea, someone's here. He's scaring me."

CHAPTER 16

E mma shifted nervously. "He says we're going to have to move."

"What?" I leaped to my feet, sending straw scattering.

"He's in the driveway. He asked where my mom was, and then he told me I better get to packing because we were getting kicked out of the house. He wants you to come talk to him."

I stared, open mouth, before looking back at the goat and the vet.

"You go figure this out. We're fine here," said AJ.

Stunned to my core, I ran out the barn and down the pebbled path. Rounding around the side of the house, I saw a black SUV sitting in the driveway. And there, leaning against the hood like the evil twin of the Jolly Green Giant, was a huge man.

He frowned as he saw me coming. "Special Agent Scarn." He flashed a badge from inside his jacket. He didn't wait for me to read it, and quickly slipped it away as his forehead creased in with a serious, no-nonsense expression.

"Can I help you?" I gasped.

"It's my understanding that you rent this place from a Douglas Glass?"

I'd heard that name before, but I still wasn't sure. No need to confirm any specifics until I learned more from Tilly.

He didn't care that I hadn't verified it. "Your lease is being revoked."

"What? Why?" She was going to have to leave the home she was so proud of? What about all of her animals?

"Looks like Douglass Glass hasn't receive any payments in the last few months."

No payments? What? That didn't sound like Tilly.

He handed me a paper and then left. His SUV spit up gravel as he backed out into the road. I glanced at the paper. It was an eviction notice.

The paper trembled in my hands, maybe catching a small breeze, but most likely from all the emotions coursing through my veins. Pam had once asked me what I'd been afraid of. Now my answer would be very different.

How was I going to tell Tilly? I could just imagine the conversation with my friend. Sure, Tilly. I'll be happy to watch your daughter. Go on to Australia. In the meantime, your sweet cherub will dye her hair blue, someone will get murdered, and then I'll get you evicted.

"That was weird," AJ said from behind me.

I turned, surprised. I hadn't heard him join us. "Why?"

"That was hokey as all get out. There's no such thing as a special agent."

"Are you sure?"

"Unless you count the fancy plastic badge you get at the bottom of Sugar Bear cereal, then, yes, I'm serious."

Who was this guy snooping around my property then? "Do I take this seriously?"

He glanced at the paper. "That looks official. But I'm pretty sure you have some rights here."

"I know we haven't been late on payments."

"You have a case then." At that he gave a half grin, half grimace. "I'm sorry this happened, but take heart in knowing your goat had two beautiful kids. All are healthy and well." He clapped my shoulder. "You need anything, let me know. In the meantime, take care of that kid over there." He gestured to Emma who was sitting on the porch with her arm around Jasper and the most forlorn look on her face.

"Look, I don't know what's going on, but you have a witness. I heard him threatening you. Don't let him scare you."

"You're right." I answered. I'd get to the bottom of this one way or another.

"Come on. Bring little miss over there. Let's go see a beautiful sight."

I smiled at him and went to the porch to grab Emma's hand. "It's going to be okay, Emma. Don't you worry."

"Promise?" she asked.

I wasn't going to let her down. "Promise."

Her fingers clenched at my fingers in confidence. Hand in hand, we followed AJ back to the barn. I glanced behind me to see Jasper following as well.

When we entered, I could hear Daisy making a soft bleat. Excited, I let go of Emma's hand and hustled over to the stall.

Momma goat stood in the clean straw, calmly chewing a mouthful of hay. On either side of her were two kids nursing. Both of the babies had their tails wiggling in circles.

"They're standing!" I gasped.

"Yep! Pretty amazing, isn't it?" AJ said, leaning against the stall door and smiling.

I couldn't believe it. I'd never seen a baby animal before, with the exception of my friend's puppy. "Look Emma!"

"Oh, they're so cute! Freckles is going to be so happy when he sees them!"

CHAPTER 17

The next morning was another rerun, with getting everyone breakfast, including Emma. I crammed the dishes in the dishwasher (wincing at the clatter when I pushed the door shut) and then examined all the animal paraphernalia the vet had left me yesterday. Things for the goats for worms, vitamins, along with long dosing syringes. I shuddered. It could wait until evening, but I was not looking forward to it. AJ said there should be enough medicine here, but if I ran out I could pick up more at the Farm and Feed.

After getting Emma on the bus, I headed to work where Polly greeted me with her usual fluttering eyelashes and smiles from over her puzzle.

"You're working on a new one!" I noted.

"Yeah, this one is supposed to be quite the brain buster."

I wandered over to check it out and saw that all the pieces were white. "Er. There's no picture?"

"Not this time. Like I said, a brain buster," she said, snapping in a piece. "Maybe, when I've finished, I'll draw a picture on top of it."

"You couldn't draw a candy cane on a Christmas tree," said her sister as she came out of the back room. "Chelsea! I'm glad to see you. How are you doing? Better?"

The slight reference to my breakdown yesterday made me wince. I nodded and smiled.

"Great!" she answered. "Well, we're going to be busy today. We just had a huge shipment of stuff from one of our local families. They're having an estate sale. Can you help me set it up?"

Of course I could. It's what I was being paid for. But I appreciated Pam's relaxed managing style.

I was unboxing the items on a table near the front door when the bird bell above the door chirped, announcing an older couple as our newest customers.

The man caught sight of me and stared. I mean a full on stare, complete with a dropped jaw. He nudged his wife who didn't understand what he meant. She turned in my direction with a casual smile. Her face paled, and she glanced at the man. Without a word, he made the sign of the cross, and then grasping his wife's elbow, he steered her back out of the store.

What in the world? Was I that scary looking? Maybe it was the dark circles under my eyes. Heaven knows I was beyond exhausted. I pushed my hair back from my cheek. I only hoped that Pam and Polly hadn't noticed. I couldn't imagine I had much job security if my very looks were driving customers away.

I wasn't sure what I could do about the exhaustion. Chores were piling up, especially with the addition of Jelly and Bean, our two baby goats. Not to mention the threat of eviction looming over my head.

Feeling a bit hopeless, I sighed and covered my face with an old magazine.

Breathe. I can get through this. I glanced at the magazine, an antique, and was immediately calmed by the cover scene.

It was of an old fashioned camper with two kids fishing in a river while the mom tended a smoldering campfire that had a pan sizzling over the top. I was reminded of the pond with a river down behind Tilly's property. Sharon had said people went on fishing trips, and her nephew was the tour guide. I decided I might need to find him. Might be nice to get a little break, and I bet Emma would like it, too.

Pam returned with another box.

"Where did you say all of this come from? An estate sale?" I asked.

"This was from the mayor's uncle, Henry McDaniel. Poor guy, the mayor can't escape tragedy, it seems. The uncle died last month. He owned the used car lot down the way, along with a recreational vehicle site. It wasn't unexpected, not exactly. After all, Henry was in his eighties and not in the best of heath. But still, I feel for Mayor McDaniel."

"Aw, what happened to his uncle, if I can ask."

"Had too many of those sneaky Petes." Here Pam mimed taking a shot of alcohol. "Drove his boat straight out to sea in a storm."

I shivered.

"Don't know who's going to take over his car business now. Was supposed to be his son." Here Polly coughed from the counter and Pam shot me an anxious look.

"His son?"

"Clint McDaniel. The one who died at your place."

I nodded. "Oh, geez."

"Course, that man was up to no good."

"Clint never was," Polly agreed, back to snapping pieces into the puzzle. Her many rings glittered from the overhead light.

"No, he never was. He was a bear in high school before he disappeared."

"I imagine Henry was happy to see him come back."

"Probably one of the only ones. Course, he was his son, what do you expect?"

"I expect Henry had all of his fingers and toes crossed that Clint was back on the right road," Pam said.

"You be careful," Polly hissed as she glanced toward a customer in the back.

Pam shrugged casually even as her gaze darted back there. "What it's true," she said, lower this time. "Don't worry. They didn't hear nothing."

Polly watched her for a second more before turning back

to me. "It's the mayor that I worry about. Clint was his cousin."

"They were close then?" I asked.

Her lips pressed together. "Closer than two fiends, and I mean that. But that was back in school. When Clint left, Mayor McDaniel got on the straight and narrow. Sometimes it takes that, separating from the ones that drag you down."

"Why are people so afraid of him? The mayor, I mean."

"Why do you think people are afraid?" Pam asked.

"Well, everyone keeps telling me I need to be nervous because Clint was found on my property. And then I got an eviction notice yesterday."

"You did? You have it on you?"

I shook my head.

Pam straightened to her full height and puffed up her dark hair. "Well, Doug Glass owns that farm out there. And he's our cousin. Why would he be evicting you?"

"The man said for late payments. But I know for a fact we weren't."

Polly rolled her eyes. "Doug Glass and Mayor McDaniel are poker buddies. Doug is a weak man. Always was. I remember he'd tattle on us as kids if we so much as snuck one piece of candy. Doug never could stand up to anything stronger than a cow sneeze, I swear. No constitution." She patted my arm. "I still got some sway with that man. He better figure this out or there won't be any Thanksgiving at our home this year."

After finishing the display, the rest of the morning was

pretty mundane and concerned dusting shelves and running laundry through the machines. That's okay. I needed something chill. My mind was already running full speed thinking about the meeting I had at lunch time with Emma's teacher, Jason Frank.

The time came all too quickly, and I soon found myself in a school hallway that was longer than any elementary school hallway had a right to be. All the doors were covered in cute posters, with the teachers' names above the doors in colorful cartoon bubble letters. I could hear kids laughing from the direction that scents of pizza and fish sticks wafted from. I assumed it was the cafeteria.

I located Mr. Frank's room and knocked.

"Come in," called a pleasant voice. It wasn't too deep— soft in the way you want bedtime stories to be read in.

I poked my head in. "Hi, there. I'm Chelsea Lawson. We have a meeting scheduled?"

"Hi! You came at the perfect time." A man about my age rose from behind the desk and strode over, hand extended. He had on a brown jacket over a t-shirt, in a mixture of professional and casual. And a definite mustache. Emma had that detail right. "I've heard a lot about you!"

"Oh, really?" I could only wonder what he'd heard.

"All good things, I promise. Did you have a chance to have lunch yet?"

"No, not yet. You?"

"Just finished. Peanut butter and jelly." He sheepishly

smiled. "I was running a little late this morning and had to go with the basics."

"I hear you," I said as I looked around. The classroom walls were plastered with cut-out colorful leaves, pencils, books, and balloons. There was a chart with gold stars on it by the door. As I went to examine it, a ruffly noise near my elbow made me jump.

On the other side of the door was a huge cage. Inside were two guinea pigs.

Mr. Frank laughed. "Those are our class babies. The kids take turns keeping them clean and giving them attention." He smiled at me. "Now, how about if you join me over here and let me get to the point."

He indicated one of the low plastic chairs surrounding a table. I instantly recoiled. He wanted me to sit in that? With an uneasy glance that brought visions of Goldilocks running amok and breaking other people's chairs, I gingerly lowered myself into the seat. I was overwhelmed with gratitude when the chair held.

Mr. Frank didn't seem to think it was weird that an adult was sitting in a kid's chair, but he didn't join me. Instead, he perched on the edge of his desk and folded his hands together. "So, I heard that Emma's mom is out of town?"

I nodded. He was probably concerned with the blue hair.

"Well, she's been talking a lot about a friend that lives at her house. A Mr. Freckles."

Oh, dear. This was about him. Invisible friends was still uncharted territory for me.

"And with what recently happened,"—here his mouth pulled into a frown—"I wanted to check in with you and see how she is really doing."

"Oh, surprisingly, she's fine." I remembered the blue hair. "I'm sure her hair was a shocker, but she did it for fun."

He laughed in a way that was meant to put me at ease. "Oh, that's fine. We see that all the time. So her concentration is okay? She's eating well? Sleeping normally?"

I nodded. "As far as I can tell, she seems happy and content. Spunky, even. How is she doing in the classroom?"

"Emma is her usual precocious self. I don't see anything to be worried about, other than the mention of Freckles. It's really not that big of a deal. Kids have imaginary friends all the time. It's better for them if we don't focus too much attention on them. I only brought it up as a concern in regards to what happened at your place. Especially since she doesn't have her mom."

"Right. Well, I'm on it. Her mom will be home soon as well."

"Okay, sounds good. If you need any help, please give me a call." With that, he stood up and leaned over his desk to rifle in a drawer. He came back with paper and a pen. Quickly, he scribbled something down. "Here's my number. Call me any time."

I tried to stand up, a little mortified at how my knees creaked. "Thank you," I said, first brushing my hair behind my ear and then accepting it.

"So, you're new in town," he started again, this time his voice a bit deeper.

I jerked my gaze up to him. His tone had changed from professional to friendly. Extra friendly.

"Yes. I like it here."

"Well, if you ever need a tour guide, I'm usually free. Maybe we could have lunch sometime, and I could show you around."

"Oh, that's awfully kind of you. I'm not sure when I'll have time. I mean, I'm the babysitter for Emma, and my car is acting up." I said, trying to figure out if etiquette was being breached.

"Sure. Of course. Bring her along."

"Bring her?" I said.

"Why not? It's just a friendly neighborly thing, and after all, I'm her favorite teacher." He grinned, raising an eyebrow. Surprisingly, his comment didn't sound as creepy as it was worded. In fact, for the first time in a while, I felt like maybe I might find my people in this new town after all.

"Oh! A fellow eyebrow archer," I sparred back, lifting my own.

"Yeah, watch this. I can do two at the same time," he said and then made a silly face with both eyebrows up.

"What a coincidence! Me too!" I imitated him, and we laughed.

"See, I told you we were kindred souls."

I laughed.

"About that lunch?" he hinted.

I wasn't sure what I wanted my answer to be. The bell rang then, signaling the end of recess. Saved by the bell.

"Not to mention," he continued. "I know where the best car mechanic is. And by best, I mean cheap."

I grinned. "We'll see," I said before heading out.

As I walked down the hallway, dodging little kids all about armpit height, I did have to ask myself. Did I really want to be saved by the bell?

CHAPTER 18

As I left the store, my car did that funny rattle again. I rolled my eyes and decided to keep ignoring it and call the Farm and Feed. I wanted to find out what happened to Sam and if he was okay.

"Farm and Feed," a woman answered.

"I just wanted to say thank you for the delivery. Was the delivery made by Sam?"

"It was. He said he was so sorry but the first time he came by your place he had a medical emergency and needed to go straight home."

"Oh, no! Is he okay?"

"Yeah." There was a pregnant pause, and then the clerk continued. "He's a dependable worker but he has epilepsy. When he says he's not well, we listen."

Poor guy. He came by and had to leave. It was just a fluke in timing.

"He's better now, I hope."

"He is, although he's taking some time off with the passing of Clint. They used to be high school buddies, and he's taking it hard. I'll pass your concern on to him."

"Yes, thank you so much."

"Okay then. Terrific. If there is anything else we can do to help, please let us know."

I said goodbye and ended the call. Then I glanced at the time. Emma was due home in a couple of hours. I had time to stop at the store and then the post office. I could use Mom's care package, that was for sure.

Family Grocery was busier than I expected. I found a spot to park in the back, grabbed one of the last baskets (an old rickety one with three working wheels and one wonky rebel) and headed inside.

I didn't need much. Some more Noodle O's, and some fresh fruit. And oddly, some dog food. Tilly had said the bag would last until she got back, but Jasper was so hungry, I wasn't so sure. Those eyes of his... I couldn't refuse him.

I brought my full basket to the check-stand and loaded the items onto the conveyer belt. There was only one checker. A huge line grew behind me, and I was grateful I'd gotten there when I did.

The checker was a young man who did not look well. He was pale, with thinning hair and puckered lips like he'd just taken a gulp of lemonade with no sugar. He sighed when he saw me and slowly began ringing my items up.

"Are you the new girl out at Tilly Miller's place?" he drawled out.

I didn't know where this was going and gave a hesitant nod.

"You know, I heard that a man died out at your place." His voice raised with each word until I was certain the people at the end of the line could hear him.

"Yes, it was very sad," I whispered, hoping to give him a hint.

"Gossip just flies around here. We don't like strangers trying to besmirch others reputation."

What was he talking about?

"Clint was a good man, you know. My dad went to school with him. They were friends."

I tried not to give a sarcastic sniff. After everything I'd heard, maybe it wasn't such a brag worthy event to be his friend. But I wasn't going to say that. Instead, I studied the gum display as if it held the key to the whereabouts of the Holy Grail.

The checker said nothing more, letting the beeps of the items going over his scanner do the talking for him. Each one sounded as disdainful as his pursed lips looked.

I glanced behind me. Was that woman judging me as well? I crossed my arms and tried not to hunker down.

The grocer sent the last item down the belt and then

stared at me. Obviously, he had no intention of bagging it up. I stormed to the end and threw my stuff into the bags. Looping them over my arm, I smiled at him. "I'm sorry that happened to your dad's friend. Have a good day." Then I spun on my heel and walked out the front door with my head held high.

The walk through the parking lot was long and lonely as I pictured the remaining customers staring at me through the window. I shoved the stuff into my trunk and tried not to fume. People obviously were confused. I needed to remember not to take it personally. I just needed to get my head in the game and head to the post office for my package after that weird nondelivery the day before. Then it was home to meet Emma.

After another engine-clattering ride, I walked up to the entrance of the post office. On the way, I caught the scent of French fries, and my stomach growled.

There was only one person at the counter before me. Although the post lady had friendly banter, they were quickly finished. I walked up to the counter, expecting the same smile. Instead, the post lady's smile fell when she made eye contact with me.

That caught me off guard. "Hi, there. I'm expecting a package, but I haven't had any mail for the last few days."

Before I could even give her my name, she stiffly nodded. "One moment, please." And then she disappeared around a shelf and through an open doorway in the back.

That was extremely odd. She didn't even know who I was. I could hear whispering and strained to listen.

A moment later she came out with a stack of mail. "The mailman said it fell between the seats. Here you go." She hesitated and then added, "If you don't get your mail again, I suppose you better come back in here and check."

"Was there a box?"

She shook her head. "Not today." And with that she returned to the back room. No asking me if there was anything else, or if she could get me some stamps. Just up and left.

I stormed out the door, ready to rip it from the hinges. They were freezing me out. Might as well tell me the mailman wasn't going to be stopping at my place anymore.

I slammed my door shut and threw the mail on the passenger seat. I didn't start the car, I didn't think I could trust myself to drive until I calmed down.

But I soon discovered that sitting in the parking lot wasn't helping. People were eyeing me as they entered the post office. I had to get out of here.

I turned the key in the ignition, planning to search for some quiet place where I could pull over. Instead, I found myself driving out of town and along the back roads, music cranked, trying to chill out.

I ended up on a road leading in the opposite way that I lived. Bright orange and yellow trees flew past me. Their leaves scattered behind my car. I found a fork and took it, and then took the next. I vaguely worried that I might not find my way back out to the main road, but the other part of me knew I could trust myself to figure it out.

There was a vacant area that opened to a large parking lot that had once served a few abandoned buildings. It looked like nobody had been here for a long time, at least not without a can of spray paint, judging from the graffiti. It was attached to another lot, and this one was filled with travel trailers. There was a huge sign that screamed in giant red letters, "End of year sale!"

The trailer lot looked like it had seen better days as well. I couldn't help but wonder what year they meant.

Past that was nothing but empty lots that were filled with grass. Trees started to creep up in the background, the kind that grew near a river.

As I drove, I wondered when the road would run out. It had the look of a dead end to it, the farther I got from town. It's funny how you can tell a dead end, even in the path of life. Experience is sometimes a tough teacher.

Sure enough, the road petered out at a dirt parking lot, with a small shack huddled at one side. The sign attached to the roof said, "Greatest river tours ever!"

Okay! I knew exactly where I was—Sharon's nephew's place. I parked in the lot, the engine clunking and rumbling before I turned it off. I climbed out and walked up to the crooked front door.

I'll admit I was standing with a stiff spine and shoulders back. I felt slightly nervous at how my treatment would be after my last two experiences.

The door's front corner dragged against the floor as I opened it. Then it gave way, and I stumbled inside.

It was an old place, you could feel it. The wood floors were dark and scarred with age, and the same wood planked walls. A man in his forties looked up from a book he was reading at the counter.

"Help you?" he asked.

"Yeah. I'm Sharon's neighbor. I think this is the place she told me about. I'm supposed to find her nephew and see if I could get a boat ride."

He stood, showing faded overalls and making the worn stool creak. "You found the right place. I'm Joss, her nephew. You're the new girl out that way?"

He was a big guy, but his age surprised me for some reason. When Sharon had mentioned her nephew I expected someone more my age. Instead, he only appeared about ten years younger than Sharon herself.

I nodded. "Yes I am."

"I heard you haven't had a very nice welcome."

That was the understatement of the year. "Not especially."

"Well, I was no friend to Clint McDaniel, and it's not your fault the way he kicked off. So I guess you're a friend of mine." He held out a calloused hand. "You in the mood for a tour?"

"I'll have a first-grader that will be with me."

"That works. I have lifejackets. You like birds?" He talked with an easy cadence, as if everything about him was a human version of the slow moving river itself.

I nodded, feeling that flicker of the same feeling that had happened with Emma's teacher. There were good people around. I needed to hold out hope that I would find them.

"It's a gorgeous river. Bring your camera. We have lots of birds and wildlife."

And so we made plans for Saturday.

Strawberries, and green grass, nightmares and red smears can knock off. I am worth being alive. I am worth being alive. I am worth being alive.

CHAPTER 19

I t's hot out. The sun is beating on my head as I walk. I have a long way to go. But I don't want to turn around. I don't want to go back. I have new shoes, and I love them. They have pink shoelaces.

There is a road sign. So many road signs. They all say the same thing. Strawberries this way. I know the place. I've been there before. A lush green carpet with tiny white flowers and sweet red berries. Fairy berries. I can eat my fill and lie in the grass and watch the white clouds tromp across the azure sky.

I'm almost there. My stomach churns in eagerness even as my sweaty hands squeeze to pick the berries. There's a noise. An unearthly noise. Should I run?

Don't you always run when you hear that noise? The noise that means the end is coming.

And so I run.

My dream, my eight-year-old legs, the strawberries take me closer to the noise. There's no escaping it. The rumble fills the air and grabs me through my Snoopy t-shirt, clenching deeper than skin. Clawing at my heart, my head, trying to get in. I scream, but the noise is bigger than that.

It's bigger than the sky.

It snuffs out the sunlight. I drop to my knees and cover my ears. The sun is gone, the colors are gone. There is nothing but the noise.

But not for long.

It never ends here. How I wish it would end here. Even in my dream I cry out, beg, plead.

Save us! Save them!

The noise doesn't answer. It doesn't care. It has no emotion. It's only goal is to eat up the sky, bringing sulfur and fire and smoke.

And death.

The strawberries vibrate on their tender green stems. The flowers are hidden in the dark shadow.

I want to go home. Home is a very long way from here.

And then it happens. Like another world intersecting ours, another dream happening in the middle of the first one, a new scene unfolds.

Earthquake. The entire world shakes. The ground booms.

Everything explodes. I'm knocked off my feet, and I fly. Only it's not like I thought flying would be. It's not free. There is no control. I face the clouds and wonder where I'm going. The clouds can't tell me.

Then I hit it. A bush. It catches me in the same way a baseball player catches a ball. I'm scooped and rolled, and then I fall to the ground.

Finally, I look up. All I see is insanity.

Fire.

Evil black smoke.

My strawberries are smashed and smeared into long red watercolor splashes.

And then I realize I'm screaming.

And not just me.

There is nothing I can do. I can't help. I can only watch from a distance as the fire's heat forces me even further away. The screams end. The fire dies to hot flickers. The watercolor splashes turn black.

And then it's over. I am alone. More alone than I was when I first got there. Birds are gone, insects. The tiny snakes in the grass.

My secret place.

It's all buried under charred soot and the remnants of an airplane.

I watch it for a while, shivering. I don't know if I'm cold. I don't know what's wrong.

The sun sets below the hill. I can see the shimmering fires now, orange footprints of death. And then there are more lights.

Red. White. Blue.

They come out of their cars and their trucks looking like Lego people. They do their job.

They find me and gasp.

I am passed from person to person as they touch my face, my arms, my back.

"Did you see this happen?" they ask.

"You are one lucky girl. So many died but you are alive."

I nod like I've heard them. I'm tired.

They put me in the back of a car. It flashes its sirens to sound important. But I know it's not. The sound is puny and has no power over life. I've seen the sound that does.

I lean back in the seat and look at the shadowy trees flashing by outside the window. Lingering around me, like the scorched scent in my clothes, is the thought, Why me? Maybe I shouldn't be here.

Maybe I shouldn't be alive.

Twenty years later, I open my eyes in a strange room, in a strange house. Once again, I struggle to rejoin real life, even as the dream, the memory, claws at my mind to keep its hooks in me.

The cow moos, and I am grateful. Keep me grounded, Rosy. Remind me I'm here and not there.

I'd discovered that healing wasn't in a straight line away from the event. Instead, it was like a spiral around a mountain. Around I go, and every time I pass the pain, I might feel the same way. But I was moving up. I was moving forward. And, bit by bit, I saw that I had changed when I came around to the memory of the event again.

At eight, I'd been afraid I wouldn't live to see another day. I'd even wrote goodbye letters, one to Mom and a couple to my friends.

Then I'd gotten sick. I needed my appendix out. I was terrified when they wheeled me back for surgery. And when I woke things had become crystal clear. I needed to earn this life. I needed to live it for those who had died.

I still didn't feel like I deserved it.

Mom worried so much about me after the airplane crash. It made her crazy how I tried to do everything right. How I tried to please all of my classmates and teachers. I remember when Mom called the counselor. She'd been standing still like a statue. A fly buzzed around her and she didn't move. That's what I remember most about that moment, that darn fly.

It landed on her arm. She said, "I can get her there tomorrow." It flew off and landed on her hair. She said okay. It lifted again, this time swooping around her head twice. She didn't notice. Instead, she locked eyes with me, her face white. I didn't see joy, I didn't see excitement.

I saw fear.

I saw preparedness.

I recognized that. Things were happening out of her control. She wanted everything to stay the same. She wanted me safe.

She was afraid I might not be.

I saw all this as she locked her eyes on me. I saw her fear.

And I never wanted to see that look on her face again.

I went to the counselor, a kind lady who listened and helped me. She was the one who had told me that I deserved happiness. That I was here for a reason. That I was good enough and didn't need to strive to earn permission to live.

That I was worthy of love.

And that I was loved.

I thank God for her.

Rosy mooed again, the goats bleated, the dog barked. There was pounding of footsteps up the stairs and then my door was flung open.

"Chelsea! Are you okay? Are we going on the river tour? It's late, and I need breakfast!" Emma demanded.

I rolled my face into the pillow and smiled despite myself. "I'm coming. Go feed your bunnies and this time don't bring them into the house."

Her footsteps thumped back down the stairs. I sat up and stretched. I wasn't living healing and truth perfectly. But I knew, the next time I came around the mountain and confronted those memories again, I'd be a little bit different than I had been.

One day at a time.

CHAPTER 20

Slowly, I got out of bed and shuffled my way to my suitcase to find clothes. By the time I made it downstairs, Emma was at the table.

"I fed the dog, the cat and the bunnies. And I couldn't wait for you anymore, so I fed myself."

I glanced over to see what her choice of food was. Peanut butter, an apple, and a box of crackers. Well, I supposed that worked. "You want milk?"

She shook her head.

"You excited for the river trip today?"

"I guess so. And tomorrow I get to see Daddy!"

That was true. David was out of town for work a lot, but he was a good guy, and a good father. I smiled at her excitement.

As she ate, I took care of the cow and goats. Then we

both showered and headed out. This time there was no hiding the rattle of the car engine. Emma gleefully pointed it out again and again.

Joss was waiting for us when we arrived.

"Good morning!" I said, climbing out.

"Morning." He rubbed his jaw. "Your car has some knocking to it. I could hear you coming all the way down the road."

I tensed. Today was supposed to be about relaxing, not thinking about new problems. "I know. I need to bring it to the mechanic."

"I don't think it's a mechanic you be needing," he said, starting over. He wiped his hands on his dirty jeans. "Pop the hood."

What? Was he going to dig into the engine right now? "I don't want to be any trouble."

"Pop the hood, I said."

He was a little brusque, but I could tell he was just a no-nonsense guy. Kind of reminded me of Sharon's attitude, now that I thought about it. Shrugging, I opened the door and did what he said.

He did some digging around, and I heard the rattle again.

"Ah. It's what I thought," he said grimly.

I was afraid to look.

He popped his head around the corner and beckoned. "Come here."

Reluctantly, I climbed out and walked around to the front. He pointed to a big metal thing, something I'd call a whatchama-call-it, but he referred to as the air filter. And then he said the one word I never expected to hear.

"Squirrels."

"Pardon me?"

"You've got squirrels hiding nuts in your engine. Those critters bury them everywhere." With that he reached in and scooped out a handful and chucked them out into the parking lot.

Squirrels. I shook my head. Joss dug around and found some more and then made one last inspection. "I think you're good now," he said. "Shut the hood and hop in."

I shut the hood but I was confused what we were hopping into.

He gestured to his SUV. "Boat's at the other end." He opened the back passenger door and tossed in some life jackets. "River runs that away. Boat's docked up past Carson's corner. We'll drive there and then float down here.

My gaze flicked to Emma who was as happy as a clam at the new adventure. Joss walked over to the driver's side. "Well, come on. I have another tour at two."

"Right." I walked over to the open rear door and peered in. Miraculously, there was a booster seat.

"Have them for my own kids," he said slowly.

I gave a brief nod and strapped Emma in. Then I climbed into the passenger side.

We bumped down the road for a few minutes. I was actually surprised when Joss pulled over to the dock. We didn't seem like we'd traveled far enough to even need a tour.

Joss seemed to read my mind. As he unpacked his gear, he explained, "River kind of goes knotty here, weaving in and out of wetlands. You'll get your money's worth, I promise."

When I saw the little boat, I wasn't sure the level of reassurance that was supposed to bring. I strapped Emma into her life jacket and shrugged on mine. It smelled of fish bait, making me wrinkle my nose.

"Oh, is that the boat!" Emma skipped ahead to the dock. I chased after her, while Joss worked on the engine. It hardly looked more than a dinghy.

"This is Baby," Joss said. "We have to be careful where we put our feet when we get in, and we need to sit still. Baby doesn't like to be rocked too hard.

I eyed him again, wondering not for the last time what I had gotten myself into. Still, this was Sharon's nephew, and I didn't think she would steer me wrong.

Joss helped us into the boat, his hand rough and leathery, and soon we were situated. He sat near the engine and then we were off.

Within minutes, we left the sounds of the road and signs of civilization. Even the power lines disappeared. Excitement bubbled inside of me. I stared ahead into the tunneling trees and dark, rippling water, and felt like I was floating into another time. Another land.

"Look, see over there," Joss murmured. His calloused finger pointed to a bare branch. "That's a red-bellied woodpecker. He's getting himself some breakfast." He threw that last line in Emma's direction.

As we watched, the bird hammered at the tree, making the distinct knocking sound.

"And over there are some egrets. Aren't they lovely? Always took my breath away."

White birds on delicate stilt-like legs stood near the edge of the river. They ignored us and stood, with slim beaks poised, hunting fish in the water.

The river was lazy, and we moved with it. Joss didn't force us faster and instead used the engine to mainly keep us in the center. I loved the expression on Emma's face. Her eyes were clear and wide and full of curiosity.

At the next bend, we came into a brighter area. Here, the trees had lost their leaves, letting in sunlight. The water reflected the sky like a dirty mirror, the clouds three shades darker, the trees brown smears. But the sun, the sun was more brilliant than ever, sending sharp flashes against the rising ripples produced by the passing boat.

"Look do you see that there?" Joss pointed.

I turned to see what had his attention. At first I thought it was a rock. And then the rock moved with a sudden spurt.

"A turtle?" Emma squealed.

He grinned. "Yeah. A common snapping turtle. You see them a lot around here."

Slicing through the water next to us were fish darting away from the shadow of our boat. I leaned, and Joss reached for my elbow. "Careful now. Don't tip the boat."

I sat back, my cheeks filling with a hot flush. "Sorry."

"No worries. I just don't want to take a dip in there. Sometimes there are snakes."

I jerked my eyes in his direction. Was he serious? His face didn't change expression. He sure seemed to be.

And then, signs of mankind. Over on the bank was garbage, plastic bags and cups. I cringed when I saw it. Joss did me one more and swore under his breath. He cast a guilty glance at Emma. "Sorry about my mouth. That makes me so mad."

"People come down here?"

"On bikes and four-wheelers. It's a well known trail. Just wish they'd keep it clean for the animals. They're leaving trash right in their living room."

As we floated by, the trail became more clear. It was a muddy slash between the trees, dug out from knobby tires, that disappeared over the hill.

"People have no respect. Leave their garbage everywhere," he grumbled again. "Just last week I was with my buddy trying to help him tow out a car out by your place. Cops called us in. The car had been there for twenty years."

"I found it!" Emma said. "Jasper and I found it!"

"Did you get it out?"

"No. It was too hunkered in there. Trees growing through it and anchoring it down. Take more time and cause more damage to move it than to let the land reclaim it."

"Where do you think it came from?"

"Serial numbers were filed off in most spots. But if I were a betting man, I'm darn sure it came through the McDaniel used car lot, eons ago. Course, by now, there'd be no paperwork. If there ever was any."

"Why do you think that?"

He shrugged. "Age of the car. How long it's been there. Dropped off like it was stolen. Cars were always being swiped off the lot back then. It was before they had any real security." He smiled. "Plus there was something else. Under one of the seats was a pen with the McDaniel logo."

"Are you serious? Did you tell the police?"

"Sure. Handed it over."

"Did you find anything... unusual?" I asked, thinking about the money.

His eyebrow flicked in my direction. "No. What else should we have found?"

"Didn't you find money?"

"Money? Nope, nothing like that." Joss didn't ask more, and I thought it was odd he didn't care. Nothing seemed important to him, yet as he scanned the shore, his eyes softened when he found birds like it was the first time he'd been down the river.

I crossed my arms and settled back. I thought Emma was going to chime in when the money was mentioned, but her attention was caught by the sounds of frogs.

"Where are they?" she asked Joss.

"Down under those rocks in there. It's thick with mayflies. That's their favorite lunch." His eyes twinkled.

Emma gave a thrilled shiver as we stared into the dark,

ripply water. It wasn't hard to imagine their wide white mouths sucking up the bugs.

The river forked. Joss guided us to drift down the one to the right. The boat gently bobbed with the current.

"How do you know which way to go?" I asked.

"Easy. I've lived here a long time." The boat rocked a bit with the new current. "That way there feeds out into the pond over at your place."

I studied the dark tunnel of trees. "That's an awful lot of water."

"Well, the river don't stop there. It splits again with a little creek run-off going to the pond. The rest of it continues down until it meets Roanoke River."

"Oh, I see."

"I want to go down it, Chelsea! Let's follow it to our place?" Emma's eyes glistened with excitement.

"Maybe next time," I said. "Now where does this go?"

"This end will eventually spill off into the town's lake. We'll drop off before that, down by my place."

"How will you get back to your car?"

"Oh, I tie my boat off down here and have someone go drop me off. Sometimes I pay a kid in the summer when business picks up." He flipped the toothpick to the other side of his mouth.

A barn roof appeared through the trees. It made me sad to see we were approaching civilization.

Joss pointed out a few more birds. My eyes weren't sharp enough to always catch them, but I nodded like I had.

"What are those?" Emma asked.

I squinted to see something silver flash through the trees. And then red flags.

"That's the RV business over there. Ol' McDaniel used to run it. Course, he's gone now, so who knows who's running it now."

I remembered processing some of his estate sale items at In For A Penny.

"I think it was supposed to be Clint who ran it," I said quietly.

"Yep, that's true. He would have run it to the ground in no time."

"You said you didn't get along with him."

"That would be an understatement. He was a bully, just like his cousin."

"The mayor," I said to clarify.

"Yep." Joss didn't seem like he wanted to waste any more energy discussing those two, so I watched the scenery. Emma trailed her fingers in the water as she searched for fish.

It was quiet. Peaceful. And piece-ful, if you know what I mean. The kind of experience that calms the mind and puts all the pieces together.

All too soon, the pier came into sight.

"Here we are," Joss said. "Hope you enjoyed your ride." He pulled over to the landing dock and held out his hand to help Emma and me up.

"I sure did. Thank you so much!" I said, and nudged Emma.

I didn't need to remind her. "I loved the turtle! Thank you for taking me to see the turtle!"

He smiled. "Any time. Glad you liked it. Tell Aunt Sharon hi from me," he said before spitting the toothpick in the water.

I promised him I would even as a strange thought bubbled inside of me. If Clint was such a bully, why would he cut and run from the very town where he was the big cheese?

But Joss didn't seem open to any more questions. When we left, I saw him trudging toward his office with our two lifejackets in hand. He turned at the doorway and waved.

I waved back. At first I wondered why he wasn't more curious about Clint's death. Then I realized that the garbage on the river bothered him more than a murdered bully ever would. And I liked that about him.

CHAPTER 21

The next morning, David (Tilly's ex husband) arrived to pick up Emma. I felt kind of proud of myself that we were so prepared. By the time he pulled into the driveway, she was as neat as a pin, which was a feat since I'd first discovered her in the goat pen rolling around with the kids.

David and Tilly got along well, and I was thankful for the sake of Emma. David was a pilot so his schedule was very sporadic. But he was a good father and spent what time he could with Emma, flying in on his days off.

He waved from the driver's seat, and Emma skipped out with pigtails flying. She was wearing her new shoes, which she swore made her run faster. I, of course, agreed. Her radiating joy was almost tangible, and I couldn't help but smile.

I waved like a maniac until they were out of sight. And then it was quiet. I had the day to myself.

It's kind of a shock to the system when life is a constant go, go, go, and suddenly it stops. Honestly, a spare couple of hours felt like forever, and I didn't know what to do with myself. I walked into the kitchen, turn around, and walked straight back out. The last thing I wanted to do was clean.

I did have a few things I wanted to check on, and now was as good of a time as any. One thing that had been bothering me since our river trip was that abandoned car. I hadn't heard anything more about it. I wondered if Officer Kennedy would tell me what they'd found.

It was a long shot, but it was all I had. I decided I would unpack a little bit while I called her. I found some coat hangers, dialed the number, put the phone on speaker, and then went over to my opened suitcase.

Of course, the cat was sleeping inside. I scooped him up and set him on the bed and then grabbed a shirt warm from his body heat. He lowered his ear in displeasure and began licking his side as if to remove the stain of me touching him.

"Hello, Officer Kennedy speaking."

"Hi, Officer Kennedy. Not sure if you remember me, but it's Chelsea Lawson from out at Tilly Miller's place."

"Of course I remember you." Her sharp tone could have cut a brick.

I cringed. I'd meant my greeting to be more as a reintroduction, but now I felt dumb. "Uh, well I had a few questions about the Pontiac out in the woods. Do you know if it's safe to go back there?"

"Yes. Why wouldn't it be?"

"I heard the car wasn't removed?"

"We decided that the cost to remove the car in its state wasn't worth it. We gathered what evidence remained and have released the site."

Well, that was nice of her to let us know. And that must be why Joss hadn't seen any money. "Did you figure out where the money came from?"

"That is still under investigation. If we need any information from you, we'll be in contact."

"How about what happened to Clint? Do you have any more information on who did it?"

"Not at this time."

"Because I'm getting an awful lot of flack from the people in town. They seem to take it personal he died out here at the farm. Almost like they think I did it. Maybe you could get the word out?"

"Ma'am, I have a lot on my plate. This world doesn't exactly revolve around you, you know."

I was astounded at her response. The whole conversation had felt like pulling teeth, but her brute insult cut me to the quick. I said some inane reply to her curt goodbye and disconnected the phone.

Numbly, I hung up the item in my hand. I needed to get out of here. I couldn't even process.

I headed to the bathroom to get ready. It was almost like I

was on auto drive. It seems I should have taken a second to deal with what I felt, because, in my distraction, I smashed my baby toe on the corner of the door frame.

Something like a screech ripped out. I didn't even sound human. Jasper came running up the stairs and skidded into the bathroom just as I hopped over to the tub. I sat on the edge, cradling my foot. Jasper's cold nose pressed against my hand as I rocked. Tears dripped down my cheeks.

In a crazy way, the injury helped. Maybe, subconsciously, I was relieved to have a reason to let myself cry. I allowed myself to indulge for a minute, gulping and squeezing my eyes.

Then, I pulled myself together, partially in thanks to my excellent nurse. I kissed Jasper's head and gave him a hug. I wasn't going to let a grouchy person get me down.

I washed my face, got myself ready, then ran downstairs for an apple.

"You be a good boy, Jasper. Keep the house safe," I said, heading out. He watched from his spot on the couch by the window as I walked to my car.

Starting the car made me smile. Joss had been right. No more weird engine rattles and no more knocks. I drove out onto the road, crunching my apple and feeling thankful I hadn't made some appointment with the mechanic for a squirrel's nest.

I decided to drive out to the place I'd passed a few days earlier, the RV business. After the conversation with Joss yesterday part of me was curious who was running it since both Clint and his father had died.

There was some apprehension that came with that decision. What if I ran into the new owner and was met with the same anger or suspicion I'd seen in other townspeople's eyes? Even worse, what if the owner was some other relative that blamed me? If the mailman was giving me a hard time, surely one of Clint's relatives would.

Maybe I wouldn't introduce myself. I'd just tell them I was looking around.

I pulled onto the lot and was immediately impressed with what felt like acres of travel homes. Who knew there were so many choices? Tan motor bodies, silver ladders going up the back to the roof, pop-outs, it appeared like the world's biggest camp out.

But instead of any evidence of people, I was greeted by an empty customer parking. I parked the car as close to the exit as possible and stared into the lot as the engine ticked.

Silence descended into the car. I reached into my purse and pulled out my pepper spray. Better safe than sorry. I scanned the area again, searching for signs of life.

Nothing. It was dead quiet.

Suddenly, my phone buzzed. I swear, I nearly peed myself. Shaking my head and half-laughing at my jumpiness, I pulled it out to check the text message.

It was from David, Emma's father. —**What's this about a Freckles that Emma keeps talking about?**

I rolled my eyes. That girl, I swear. I texted.—**It's her new imaginary friend. Her teacher said the less we react to it, the less it will be a thing.**

He sent back a thumbs up. I dropped the phone into my purse and grabbed the door handle. I blew out a gust of air. Here goes nothing. Then, lifting my chin in determination, I climbed out and locked the door.

The air was brisk, but instead of smelling fresh, it carried the scent of oil and gasoline. I walked over to the office, side-stepping a pile of fast food wrappers along the way. To the side of the office was a pair of muddy tracks, like those made by an ATV.

The lights were off in the office, but I still knocked on the front door. I tried the doorknob, and it was locked. Cupping my hands to block out the light, I peered inside the modular.

There were the usual desks filled with stacks of folders and computer monitors. Nothing inside gave me a sign if they were simply closed for lunch, or if they were closed for good.

I walked back down the steps as the wind picked up and tugged at my jacket. I pulled it close and slowly walked out into the parking lot. I surveyed the rows of trailers. It was as if even the birds had abandoned this place. The only sound was a faint hush from the highway.

Then I saw it. A stack of books sitting on the metal steps of one of the RVs. They looked like paperbacks, in fact I recognized one as a mystery novel. What were they doing out here? They could get destroyed in the weather. I walked over, curious.

The cover of the top book fluttered in the wind. As I got closer, I could see I was right. It was a stack of mysteries. I picked up the first one to read the title and then looked in both directions. Who had left them here?

Just then, the trailer's door opened. I froze in surprise as a man in a red coat bounded out. One side of his blond-white hair was slicked straight on end from a heavy night's sleep.

We stared at each other in shocked silence. I honestly can't tell you who was more freaked out.

"Hello?" I said, a little apprehensively.

His face turned white, and his eyes looked like two runny eggs, what with the dark circles and bags under them. "Denise!" he gasped, staggering back.

I didn't have a chance to respond, because he blurted out again. "I'm sorry, Denise. It wasn't my fault!"

"Wait, what?" I asked.

He sprang down the metal steps, making the whole trailer shake. When he passed me, he visibly cringed, like he didn't want to touch me. The next thing I knew, he raced around the RV, and then he was out of sight.

CHAPTER 22

What the heck just happened? Who was that guy?

He'd left the RV door open, and I could see personal items inside. What looked like piles of dirty clothing. Shoes. More books. He must be living in the travel home. Did the owners know?

What owners, Chelsea? I asked myself. I checked for him again before running back to the parking lot with a few glances over my shoulder. His expression when he'd first seen me was like he'd seen a ghost so I wasn't too afraid he'd sneak up on me. But you could never be too sure.

I pointed the key fob at the car as I ran, unlocking it. As soon as I jumped in, I locked the doors. My heart was thumping. Okay, what should I do next? Call the police?

But what would I say? I didn't know who he was, and he

really might have permission to be there. The more I thought about it, the more that idea felt a little uncomfortable to me, almost like I was meddling.

Well, I couldn't just sit here, trying to decide. I was a little too rattled to go home, so I decided to head for In For A Penny. Being around safe people was what I needed. It wasn't so much as coming across a guy living in an RV that had me so rattled. It was the expression on his face when he said it wasn't his fault. And Denise... he'd called me Denise. Someone else had done that before. I wracked my brain trying to remember.

And then it hit me. The man staring at me from inside the car when I was crossing the crosswalk.

Weird and weirder.

The drive back to town didn't help calm down the Ferris wheel of weird thoughts happening in my mind. I almost wished for a rattling squirrel's nest to distract me.

Cedar Falls was busy as ever. It seemed like everyone was out shopping this Sunday, and it took me a bit to find a parking spot. Eventually I did, nosing in my car. I grabbed my purse and hurried down the sidewalk for the thrift store.

The little bird alarm trilled as I walked inside the store. I was hit with the fragrance of old books with their welcoming well-thumbed page-scent. Several new stacks sat on a table to the immediate right of the door.

I took a deep breath and felt my shoulders relax. Books were so grounding. They promised so many things, adventure, comfort, friendship, and escape.

There were a few customers milling about, making their own light shopping sounds of picking things up and setting them back down. As usual, Polly was behind the counter with an almost complete puzzle and a slice of pizza on a paper plate before her.

Did the sisters ever take a day off? Ironically, my question was answered when I asked Polly where Pam was at.

"Pammy's at home," said Polly, tucking a gray wisp behind her ear. She nudged her glasses up her nose and stared at the puzzle pieces. Her tongue darted out in concentration. After picking up a piece, she glanced up. "Where you should be. What's going on with you?"

"What do you mean?" I asked, amazed at her deducting skills.

Her thickly mascaraed eyes gave a few blinks. "Well, dear, it's Sunday. Here you are at work, and your eyes are puffy. Something must be wrong. Are you okay, love?"

I shook my head as I pulled up a stool.

Polly clucked her tongue and disappeared into the backroom. A moment later, she came out carrying two steaming mugs.

"Here. I made you some hot cocoa. My grandmother always made this for me when I felt especially bad."

I glanced down to see the drink was from a mix, the kind with the tiny miniature marshmallows. They bobbed along the top, melting in a foamy trail.

"Thank you," I said and took a grateful sip. I hadn't had this since Mom had made it for me as a kid.

"Now, why don't you tell me what's going on. Besides ol' Clint deciding to kick off at your place."

"Well, you know they think he was murdered, right?" I whispered.

Polly nodded and took a sip. "I heard."

"Ever since then I've been treated like an outcast from everyone at Cedar Falls. Like I'm the one who did it. And today I got yelled at by the officer in charge of the investigation."

Polly took a sip and then neatly wiped off her cocoa mustache. "Who is that, dear?"

"Officer Kennedy," I answered glumly.

"Oh, Officer Kennedy? Don't worry about her. She's all bark and no bite unless you're the bad guy. Then she'll snatch you up right quick. She's just no nonsense and has a lot on her plate right now. I'm sure she didn't mean it."

I thought about that. Officer Kennedy did say the world didn't revolve around me. It wasn't a nice comment, but it could be interpreted as another way of saying she had problems of her own.

"Besides, I have a bit of an inside scoop. She's been getting a lot of heat regarding Clint's death."

I peeked over my mug. "How do you know that?"

Polly raised her chin, making her long earrings dance. "It's Mayor McDaniel, dear. He's out for blood."

"Why is the mayor so vindictive about it?"

"I'm not sure. Things turned on their ear when the medical examiner ruled Clint's death a murder. I think Mayor

McDaniel was much happier with thinking it was simply an overdose. He's been trying to keep things all hush hush, and you just can't do that with a murder investigation. And that type of digging is liable to bring up a few skeletons with it. It doesn't help that he's up for reelection."

I picked up a puzzle piece and tried to fit it in. "I heard that there was someone running against him."

Polly glanced around to see where the customers were before leaning in to whisper, "Yeah. Laura Owens. I've known her from when she was a little girl. She'll give him a run for his money, that's for sure."

"Maybe that might be a good thing." It felt like a bold statement to say, in this Mayor-ish climate.

"The McDaniel family has been running this place for a while. Too long, some are thinking. And just like that, two are gone, and the mayor's reelection is up in the air." She snapped one more piece into the puzzle.

I took another sip. Should I tell her about the trailer park?

"Go on. Tell me," Polly encouraged, not even looking at me.

Geez. How could she tell? This woman's insight was starting to freak me out. "I went to the RV lot today, the one that Henry McDaniel owned."

"Well, what were you doing clear out there, for?"

"I was curious. Like you said, the McDaniel family has taken a hit. I wondered who was running the business."

"And what did you find out?"

"It didn't seem like anyone was."

"Well, I could have told you that. There's been some kerfuffle regarding Henry's will, especially now with his son Clint gone. They'll sort it out, I'm sure. I suspect it will all end up going to the mayor."

"I did see one person though, a man. It took me off guard. He appeared to be living in one of the trailers. He scared me as much as I scared him, I think." I frowned. "He called me by some strange woman's name."

"Really? How peculiar. What did he look like?"

I did my best to find words to describe him without using adjectives like rumpled and sleepy. "Blond-white hair. Bulky red jacket. Huge feet."

"Odd, so odd. Blond hair, huh? I think I know who you are talking about. Was he about this height?" She held her hand up to her eyebrows. Polly was a tall woman so it was still taller than I was. I nodded.

"Hmm. That sounds an awful like Sam Setter."

I raised my eyebrows. Was that who I thought it was? "Does he work at the Farm and Feed?"

"You got it. Been at the job for most of his adult life."

At that, my eyebrows practically shot off my face. "Are you serious?"

"Yeah. You know him?"

"He was supposed to make a delivery at my house the morning Clint died."

The lines around her mouth crinkled deeper with a frown. "That doesn't sound good. Now what name did he call you?"

"He called me Denise."

"Very peculiar. For some reason, that's ringing a bell, but I can't quite put my finger on it." She rolled her eyes. "Where is Pammy when I need her? She has a better memory about this sort of stuff."

"I wonder why he was staying out there?" I said.

"I'm not sure. I guess you have to add it to your list of mysteries." She harrumphed. "And you do seem to be collecting quite a few." She put in another puzzle piece. "Some people are talented, I suppose."

I laughed, feeling kind of sick.

"There's just one thing I want to know," she said, her eyes focusing sharply on me.

"What's that?"

"Just how many dead bodies are you planning to find?"

CHAPTER 23

Talented, Polly had said. Well, finding mysteries and dead bodies was a talent I wished I didn't have. I headed back home determined to think that the day wasn't a total loss. In fact, I might jump in the bath with a glass of wine, and regroup since Emma was out of the house.

But before I did that, I knew I needed to call Officer Kennedy again. My stomach clenched at the thought since our last phone call was less than ideal. I wasn't going to be able to relax until it was done. Sighing, I dialed. Something was going on and things were starting to feel like—even if they weren't exactly falling into place—they were pieces of the same puzzle.

"Hello Chelsea. Yes, I remember you," Officer Kennedy volunteered when she answered. As usual, her tone was as dry as a box of Saltines.

"Err, hi, again. Listen, I might have more clues for you."

"Terrific. And what is it this time?"

I couldn't tell if she was being sarcastic or interested. I forged on. "So, on the morning that Clint died I was supposed to get a hay delivery."

"Okay."

"The guy never showed up. I actually had to call the Farm and Feed because I was so desperate for alfalfa. At the time, the people who worked there didn't know where he was either. Well, I might have found him today at the RV lot. I think he's living in one of them."

"Who is this guy?"

"His name is Sam Setter."

"Why did his absence stand out to you?" Her voice was razor-edged, and I could tell she was paying attention.

"The funny thing is that our back gate was opened like a delivery had been made. And we found a hay hook. He really might have been there that morning."

"Interesting. Thank you for letting me know. I'll definitely be checking that out."

We hung up. I had to admit, I felt slightly vindicated.

When I arrived home, I discovered AJ was there for some reason. Now what? Thoughts for an immediate bath dissipated in imaginary lavender-scented steam.

Jasper watched me anxiously from the front window. I threw my purse on the buffet and let him out, and then walked to the barn where I assumed the vet was at.

I found AJ sitting on a bale of hay with one of the kids in his arms.

"Oh, hi," he said with an easy grin. His flannel shirt was unbuttoned, showing a clean white t-shirt underneath. "I just wanted to stop by and check on my newest patients. This one sure is a fighter." He cuddled the kid against his chest. "What did I call you? Kangaroo Jack?"

"You think so?" I asked, leaning against the stall door. Jasper bumped past me and into the stall to give Daisy and the other kid a thorough sniffing.

"I do. By the way, I gave them their second dose of medicine, so you don't have to worry about that again."

Hallelujah! It felt like the sky had opened and the sun was finally shining on me today. No more goat snorts of medicine all over my clothing. "Thank you so much!"

"Not your favorite chore, huh?"

I shook my head, as Daisy's particularly charming habit of tipping her head so the liquid gushed out the side, while Jasper tried to lap it up ran through my mind. "That would be a strong no."

AJ laughed. He carried the kid back to the stall and gently set him down. Jasper immediately ran his nose along the kid's spine. The little goat arched its back and bleated in pleasure.

"Wow, that dog is getting a little chunky, isn't he?" AJ noted. He reached down to feel the dog's ribs.

I glanced at Jasper. He did look thicker. "He's always hungry." I said.

"How much are you feeding him?"

"So, I started him out on two scoops—"

"Perfect." AJ scratched Jasper's side.

"But his bowl was always empty. And he was so sad when he looked at me."

AJ laughed. "Oh, he's working you. He knows an amateur when he sees one."

"Amateur at what?"

"At the puppy pout. It's one of their superpowers to get what they want." He rubbed the dog's chin. "Are you milking her sympathy, boy? Are you a pro?"

Jasper's tongue lolled out in his doggy smile. His shaggy tail wagged contentedly.

"Put him back on the two scoops. Not one bit more. And no table scraps. Don't fall for his begging. He doesn't like it, but it's what's best for him."

"Oh, I didn't hurt him, did I? By overfeeding him?"

"Nah. He's fine. He'll just have sore feelings for a bit once he realizes he was caught and you aren't going to fall for his tricks any more."

"Oh, Jasper!"

AJ glanced down and brushed off his pants. Unidentifiable hair clung to them, some from the goats, some from whatever animal he'd seen before coming here. A few hairs floated off, but most stubbornly clung to the canvas material.

"Not coming off too well," he said with a frown.

I laughed.

AJ gathered his bag, and then I walked with him back to his car. We shared some small talk, nothing too serious. It was nice to make some new memories at the farm that didn't involve dead bodies.

"Don't forget to pick up those supplements for the goats. They really need them. The Farm and Feed carries a nice brand."

"The Farm and Feed! They have everything!"

"They really do. Everything from vaccines to tranquilizers. And diet dog food!" he sent to Jasper.

The dog was deliriously happy with the attention and ran around the vet's legs, nearly tripping him.

We reached AJ's car, and he opened the door and tossed his bag in. A weird odor came out, something sharp and medicinal. I wrinkled my nose.

AJ noticed. "Yeah, doesn't smell great. Spilled a bottle of oral equine medicine back there." He didn't seem to be in a hurry to leave. "You been down to the coffee shop?" he asked, leaning on the door.

"Which one? Sweet Buns? That place is great."

"I like that one. Of course, I half-live on the coffee at the convenience store since they're open twenty-four hours."

"Your job has some crazy hours."

"That's an understatement." He laughed, slowly swinging his door back and forth. "Well, maybe I'll be seeing you again soon."

"That would be great."

"Maybe this time with no sick animals involved."

A zing of surprise—*and was that excitement? That's*

excitement, Chelsea—shot through me. But before I could respond, my phone rang.

It was Tilly. Now I was doubly caught off guard.

"Uh, I have to take this," I said, backing up.

"Oh, yeah. Sure." AJ flushed, and started to jump in his car.

"But I'd love to!" I shot out like a lightning bolt, before hitting answer.

"Yeah?" He gave a crooked grin.

I gave him a thumbs up, and he slammed the door.

"Hello? Tilly?"

"Chelz, is everything okay? Is Emma with David?"

I waved as AJ backed out of the driveway. "Yeah, everything is great. She'll be home tonight. How about with you? What's going on?"

"Oh, it's been absolutely insane over here. You can't believe the heat! Only springtime here but it's a scorcher. Anyway, I talked with Douglas Glass. You know, my landlord? Apparently there's been a mistake, and he says he's so sorry."

I smiled, wondering how much Pam and Polly's threat of no Thanksgiving dinner had to do with it. "That's great news. Hey, guess what, Daisy had twins!"

"She did?" There was a static-filled pause. "I guess I have more to learn about animal husbandry than I thought."

"You didn't tell me she was pregnant!"

"I thought she had more time, so it wouldn't matter."

"Oh. Well, everyone is fine and healthy."

In the background, I heard someone talking to Tilly. "Just

a second," she said to the person. And then, back to me, "Thank you again, Chelz! I'll call Emma later tonight!"

She ended the call. I half-smiled, happy to know things were going so well for her, and shoved the phone into my pocket. Slowly, I slunk down on the front steps and then surveyed the farm.

Quiet again. Restful even, as the breeze tousled the yellow grass and tall clover.

That is, until Jasper took off barking for the orchard.

CHAPTER 24

"Jasper!" I screamed, flying up from the step.

He didn't hear me. Either that or he didn't care. He definitely wasn't turning back. Now he was just a dark splotch running through the field.

I wasn't saying very nice words when I stormed into the house. I wasn't going after him this time without the leash. At the last second, I grabbed my pepper spray.

Slamming the door behind me, I ran down the steps and through the yard. Rosy watched me curiously as I sprinted along the fence and past the barn. I was pleasantly surprised when I reached the apple trees that I was still going strong. No stitch in my side, nor any of that out-of-breath nonsense that had plagued me so recently.

Amazing.

Still, the tall grass slowed me down. The lower half was

matted by the rain and wind, and it snagged my shoelaces. I pushed through and hurried into the trees on the other side. As I walked my mind ping-ponged between Jasper being so ornery and something that AJ had said. It was really nagging at me. Was it the fact that he hinted about getting together? I shook my head. No, that wasn't it.

I could hear Jasper now just ahead of me. His barks sounded like he was down by that old Pontiac.

The woods smelled loamy and damp as autumn settled in for good. I climbed over the old log grimacing as my hand slipped on the slimy wood.

As I slid my other leg over, it occurred to me what it was that AJ had said. My mouth opened in excitement. That was it!

Just then, Jasper's barking reached a fevered pitch, driving all thoughts from my mind. I slowed down to disentangle my shoelace from a straggling twig and tried to listen.

Something was wrong. He didn't normally go crazy like that.

Then I heard a voice. A man's. "Shh, Jasper. It's me. You know me buddy."

I froze in mid-step, my blood turning to ice. Slowly, I pulled my phone out. Holding my breath to listen, I dialed nine and then one. My finger hovered over the final one, while my other hand reached for the pepper spray.

Jasper did seem to recognize the man because the dog quieted down. I crept a little closer watching the forest floor for sticks that might crackle and give me away.

"It's all gone. Every bit of it. Where'd it go, buddy? Did she take the money? Doesn't she know I got revenge for her death? I'm tired of being haunted. Why did she come back and haunt me, buddy?"

I peered through the trees, their branches bare of leaves, their twiggy ends spindly black like witches fingers. Holding my breath, I ducked lower, trying to see. A red coat. Stunned, I covered my mouth.

Sam.

My heart slammed in my chest. Quickly, I backed up, my shoes digging into the wet leaves. At the fallen log I decided to call Officer Kennedy instead of finishing the emergency call.

"Fancy hearing from you again," she said. This time the sarcasm cut through like a trail of dish soap into a puddle of oil.

"Sam Setter is at the car in the woods. He knows about the money," I whispered. Adrenaline had me nearly gasping.

"Chelsea?" The officer's voice instantly became grave. "Are you in trouble? Where are you?"

"I'm going back to the house. But he's here at the abandoned car. He's talking something about revenge. Can you come get him?"

I heard her call a code out, I was assuming into her mic, and she gave an address. Then she was back on the phone. "I want you out of there. Lock your doors. Don't come out until you hear from me again."

"But my dog is there with him."

"Sam won't hurt the dog. Get up to the house. You being in the vicinity compromises not just your safety, but ours as well."

"Got it. I'm on my way."

"We have this handled. It's over, Chelsea." We hung up, and I climbed over the log.

She said it was over. Except it wasn't.

At the edge of the forest, I turned around for one last look. I hoped beyond everything to see Jasper's sweet face, that somehow he'd known I was there and followed me out.

There was nothing but vacant space between the trees. I wanted so badly to call for the dog, but I was afraid to alert Sam.

My heart was heavy as I trudged back through the orchard and up to the house. I swear, I'd never prayed so hard as I did for that dog.

One thing I knew was that I needed some answers. You couldn't send me back to the house by myself and without my dog without understanding why. I had clues, lots of them. And, like Polly, I wanted to finish the puzzle.

I opened the door to the emptiest house that ever existed. No doggy kisses greeted me. I was scared. It was hard to trust what Officer Kennedy said.

Pull yourself together, Chelsea.

I sank to the foyer floor with a spiral notebook to make a list of the puzzle pieces I had.

There was the abandoned car full of money.

Lots of money.

A car that might have come from McDaniel dealership, especially with the pen on the floor board. The car dealership had been run by Clint McDaniel's father. Clint was a known partyer and trouble maker twenty-odd years ago. And then he left town for some inexplicable reason.

Sam and Clint used to be high school friends. The Farm and Feed employee said that Sam was taking time off since he was destroyed by Clint's death.

Tom from the bakery told me that he felt for Sam because the poor guy's girlfriend of his youth had been murdered. He never recovered.

But how did all those pieces tie together?

I stared at my list.

Wait a minute...

My jaw dropped open. I'd had the key all along and hadn't realized. It was in the old news story that Sharon had told me. The one about the bank robbery in town, where the robbers had killed the teller after they had her open the vault.

Was it so far fetched to think that Clint had robbed the bank and, in the process, killed Sam's girlfriend? And afterwards Clint's family, specifically Mayor McDaniel, had forced him to leave town.

And Sam finally got his revenge when Clint recently returned to town. How did he do it? By using a tranquilizer injection from the Farm and Feed where he worked.

Walking freely on Tilly's property was no problem for Sam. He was friends with Jasper. The Farm and Feed employee mentioned that Sam talked about the dog all the time.

But if Clint had robbed the bank and then been forced to leave town, why was the car—still full of money—abandoned in the woods? That didn't make any sense. Wouldn't Clint have taken the car when he left town?

Further more, why was Clint in the barn at all? Was it just a coincidence that it was the same morning that Sam was supposed to be here dropping off the alfalfa?

The questions battered me, and I couldn't process anymore. Worry over Jasper was using all my head space and running my thoughts ragged.

The next twenty minutes dragged by like it was three years. I didn't move. My butt hurt from sitting on the hard floor, my back hurt, but all I could think about was Jasper.

So when I heard barking on the front porch, I can't explain the bolt of joy that charged through me. It was the best sound in the world. I ran to the foyer serenaded by an orchestra of nails scratching on the door. Eagerly, I flung it open.

It was Jasper all right. Tongue lolling, happy Jasper.

And right behind him was Sam.

I started to slam the door shut, when the man lunged to shove it open. "Wait! Stop! I need to talk to you!"

The movement startled Jasper who began barking again. I pushed with all my weight against the door. My feet skidded along the wood floor as Sam slowly forced me back. At the last second, I released the door and turned to run. I hoped the unexpected action would take him off guard but he was too quick. Before I'd gone two steps, his hand clamped down on my arm.

"You're real," he breathed.

"Let go of me!" I demanded. I wasn't going to show any fear, and I wasn't about to back down.

His hand dropped from my arm as if it had been scalded. I took a cautious step back, my hands balled into fists. Then I remembered and pulled out my pepper spray. I held my wrist to keep my hand steady. "Get out of here!"

He took a step back with his hands up. "Wait! Just give me a chance to explain, Denise!"

"Stop calling me that! My name's not Denise!"

He recoiled as if I'd slapped him. His mouth gapped like he was trying to form words in another language.

"I'm not Denise!" I insisted again. "My name is Chelsea."

This time, when he finally spoke, it was in a croak. "I'm so sorry. I'm so very sorry. I've not been well. I—I got confused." With that Sam turned and stumbled down the stairs.

I lunged for Jasper's collar when it looked like the animal might follow him, and then slammed the door, locking it tight. Then I leaned against it, heart pounding.

I needed to call someone. 911. Officer Kennedy.

I yanked the phone out, nearly dropping it. I tried to dial with trembling fingers. Just then I heard a ruckus out in the front yard. I ran to the window, where Jasper had already jumped on the couch. I gasped to see Sam on the ground with Officer Kennedy's knee in the middle of his back.

"Hands over your head!" she screamed. She soon had his hands wrestled behind him and handcuffed.

I sank to the couch, my head hitting the cushioned back. Fingers of relief fluttered through me, feeling like chills, like weakness. I took long gulping breaths. I had no idea how the cop came to be here, but I was so, so grateful.

A moment later, footsteps thumped up the porch steps followed immediately by pounding on the door. "Chelsea? Are you okay?"

I sprang to my feet and ran to wrench it open. Seeing her face nearly undid me, and I almost collapsed into her arms for a hug.

Her hand was on her gun, and she looked anything but huggable.

"Thank God you're here! How did you know he would come?"

Officer Kennedy turned to look at Sam, who lay sprawled out on his stomach. "I had a gut feeling I needed to check on you when we got to the car and the dog wasn't there. My intuition told me Sam might be hiding."

Another officer popped up from behind the barn and yet another by the mailbox.

I wanted to kiss them all.

Apparently Jasper felt the same because he raced over to leap up on one and then the other, and then the next, trying to give them enthusiastic puppy kisses.

"What am I being arrested for?" Sam yelled with a face full of dirt.

"I heard you," I called to him. "I heard you say you got your revenge."

When his eyes caught mine, his bravado slipped away. "Denise. Denise. I'm so sorry."

"What are you sorry for, Sam?" I asked.

"I'm sorry he killed you. You weren't supposed to get hurt. He was supposed to just take the money and go."

"Clark!" yelled Officer Kennedy. "Mirandize him." She turned back to me and closed her eyes tightly.

"I'm sorry," I said.

"No. You're good."

Officer Clark stood Sam up. "You are under arrest for the murder of Clint McDonald. You have the right to remain silent." He continued to read the rights.

I turned to Officer Kennedy. "You have the proof?"

"Yeah, along with a whole slew of other charges including attempted kidnapping. He's going to be locked up for a while."

"I knew it! Something occurred to me today. I meant to call you."

"You know, Chelsea, there's a part of me that really regrets giving you my phone number."

"I'm sorry. Do you want to know what it is?"

"Please tell me."

There it was again. Was it sarcasm or interest? I shook my head. I'd probably never be able to read her. "So I remember when you said that Clint had died of an overdose. You specifically said it was a tranquilizer, remember."

She arched an eyebrow. "I do."

"I just found out you can buy it at the Farm and Feed where Sam works. And I heard Sam say twice that he got revenge for the death. Now we just need to prove whose death he's talking about."

Her eyes twinkled. "I think we have an idea."

I must have looked uncertain because she sighed. "Look, if you want to know, I suggest you follow his trial." With that, she walked down the stairs and stalked over to Sam, who was still staring at me.

And then he yelled, "I've wished every day that it never happened. I've lived it over and over. It's been a nightmare. I hope you can forgive me."

He had tears in his eyes and real anguish on his dirt-smeared face. And my heart softened a touch. After all, I knew a little bit about living nightmares. I slowly lifted my hand, hoping that simple gesture was enough to give him peace. He had a long road ahead of him. I hoped this time he would find his way.

CHAPTER 25

"Come on, let's go." The police marched Sam down the driveway where several cop cars had appeared.

I shut the door slowly. Bolted it and check it twice. And then I sank to the floor where Jasper rested his head in my lap. He gave a whistley dog nasal sigh.

Sam's last words kept ringing through my mind. "He was supposed to take the money and go. You weren't supposed to get hurt."

Sam obviously had me confused with someone else. And it had to be the bank teller.

It happened a long time ago, but could there be something about the bank robbery on the internet? Sharon said it had made a huge impact on the town. And a huge impact meant there had to be some sort of lasting story? Right? Even if it was over twenty years old.

I grabbed my phone and typed in Cedar Falls, followed by the words, bank robbery. Despite my reasoning, I still was surprised when I saw there were several links. I sucked in an excited breath, and Jasper looked up with concerned eyebrows. I rubbed them down. "It's okay, buddy. I'm looking to see what this is all about. Don't you want to know? I know I do."

He rested his head on my knee after sniffing my phone. Apparently, he wanted to see as well.

I clicked the first link.

It opened to a grainy photo. Someone had take a shot of the original newspaper article and then uploaded it. The headline was blatant and to the point.

Teller Murdered in Bank Robbery Gone Wrong.

I greedily started to read when my gaze dropped down to the included picture of the teller.

And that's when my whole world shook to its core. Because the person in the picture was me.

I grabbed the buffet table leg to steady myself. Jasper sat up. His tail thumped against the wood floor as he shoved his nose in my face. I couldn't even speak to calm him down.

When I say it was me, I don't mean a little bit like me. I mean her face was exactly like mine, down to the dimple in my cheek and with the same crooked eyetooth.

I felt woozy and fanned my face. I'd seen a lot of strange things, but this... this was too much. I leaned my head against the wall. What was even happening? How could this be?

It wasn't just Sam who had mistook me for her. I

squeezed my eyelids tight as I remembered the older couple who entered the thrift store and made the sign of the cross when they saw me before running out the door. There was the man at the crosswalk, who screamed the name of Denise while staring at me in disbelief. Even Tom and Sharon had said I reminded them of someone from long ago.

My fingers started to tingle, coupled with an itchy stranglehold in my chest. I recognized the feeling immediately as the beginning of a panic attack, something that had happened to me a lot during the first year after the airplane crash. Slowly I breathed in through my nose and concentrated on stroking the dog's back. Jasper blasted me with warm pants.

It's okay. People look like one another. It's a strange world.

Slowly I opened my eyes, and when I was ready, I glanced at the article again. It was from twenty-three years ago. I was five at the time that she died.

As I studied the woman's face, cold chills ran over me again. Her name was Denise Smith, and she was younger than I was now at the time of her death. Looking at the pictures was like looking at an old college photograph of myself. Her hair was tucked up in a bun, but I had the same sleek look when I pulled mine back into a ponytail.

The picture quality wasn't great, but even her eyes appeared to be the same dark color as mine. I now fully understood what Sam meant when I overheard him at the car saying he was being haunted.

The article spoke of a blue Pontiac as the get-away car. In capital letters, it asked the public to keep an eye out.

There was one more thing. A description of the get-away driver. The news story said that the robbers separated, with one throwing the bag of money in the car and then leaving on foot.

And suddenly, it all made sense. The final piece of the puzzle clicked in.

When I read the description of the driver—white blond hair—I couldn't believe that Sam hadn't been caught in all these years.

He was the driver. He'd driven the car one way while Clint ran the other. He must have left it hidden in the woods. This was why he felt so much guilt all these years.

Then I realized why neither of them had been caught. The McDaniels ran the town. They orchestrated Clint leaving. They most likely hushed the story. After all, the mayor had political ambitions and couldn't let a little murder and bank robbery get in the way.

I stared at the picture again. I just couldn't get over how much she looked like me. I didn't recognize the last name. She was no family relation that I knew of.

Fingers trembling, I saved a snapshot of the teller so I could send it to Mom. It would freak her out, I knew it would. Still I had to share it with her. This was all too strange.

My phone vibrated in my hands, interrupting the photo background and scaring me. It was Polly. Surprised, I pressed the answer key.

"Hi, Polly,"

"Oh Chelsea! I'm so glad you answered. Are you okay? Pammy and I have been worried sick!"

So they'd already heard. Gossip sure got around fast in this little town. "I'm fine. Everything is under control."

"Under control? You just are so brave. Brave I tell you! To think that man came into your house. I can't believe it."

"It was a little freaky," I admitted, holding out my hand to look at it. It was still shaking.

"And you were alone with him at the trailer park! Can you imagine what could have happened there?"

"Well, he ran away from me. He was more scared than I was. I wonder what he was doing out there. He has a home, doesn't he?"

"Oh, sure he does. You didn't hear? It was actually Clint's trailer. I have no idea what Sam was doing at his place. Looking for something, I suppose."

"Why did Clint live in the travel trailer?"

"Well, I'd heard when he returned to Cedar Falls, he was quite down on his luck. Lost his entire fortune in a bad investment. I heard he only returned to Cedar Falls to get his feet back under him."

That's right. Tom had told me that as well. Getting his feet back under him could also translate into him realizing the stolen money had to be out there somewhere. Clint must have pressured Sam into telling him where.

Maybe they were meeting in the barn so that Sam could lead him to the money. And Sam killed him there as some sort of weird homage to Denise, since this is where I lived, and he thought I was Denise.

It must have horrified Sam when he first saw me. Here I was living so close to where he'd stashed the money and car. No wonder he'd thought I'd come to haunt him. Maybe he'd hoped, with Clint dead, the nightmares would end.

Like I said, I was no stranger to nightmares. But I knew they didn't end that way.

Polly continued, cutting through my musing. "Anyway, we heard through one of our good friends who knows the attorney representing Sam that Sam is going to plead guilty." She sighed. "It's just such a tragic story."

"I agree. But maybe the fact that Sam is pleading guilty shows that he's finally on the right path."

"Yes." I heard furtive whispering, and Pam urged, "Tell her! Tell her!"

Polly took in a deep breath. "Chelsea, you know I don't want to upset you, especially at a time like this, but there was something we thought you should know."

I tensed. "Okay."

"Remember the name you said that Sam called you? And I told you that it rang a bell? Well, I asked Polly and she reminded me that was the name of Sam's girlfriend. His late girlfriend."

"I know about it. I found the story online."

"And did you read it?"

"I sure did."

Polly hesitated. In the background, Pam encouraged her

again. "Anyway, we think we know why he called you that. Polly still has the actual clipping, and honestly you look an awful lot like his girlfriend. It's quite remarkable."

"I noticed that as well."

"The likeness is so similar that we've actually had a few people ask about you."

"Okay." I wasn't sure where this was going, but suddenly I didn't like it.

"So, we both think it would be best, Pammy and I, if you took a tiny leave of absence. Just until this whole thing with Sam is cleared up. We like a bit of notoriety, but this seems like it might be over our heads."

"Why? What's happening?"

"We've had people wonder if poor Denise is haunting our place or if this is a case of reincarnation twenty years later. We wouldn't mind so much but business has been down."

I wondered if business wasn't really down because Mayor McDaniel put the out word for everyone to avoid the thrift store. After all, look what happened between me and the mailman. Still, I wasn't going to argue with them. "I'm sorry to hear that."

"Just for a week or so. You probably need some time to sort yourself out, as well. And really, if you haven't seen the picture, you need to look it up."

We said goodbye and ended the call. I rubbed my temple. Honestly, I felt about as low as one could get. Did I still have a job? Was I about to be run out of town? Was having a resemblance to a woman dead twenty years ago really enough to warrant this kind of treatment?

Outside, Rosy mooed, and the goats bleated, and I was once again reminded that I needed to get my chores done. Emma was going to be home any minute. Real life was crashing my pity party.

I found my purse from where I'd flung it a life-time ago when I'd seen the vet was here, and pulled out my wallet. That empty, needy feeling gripped me as I searched for the photograph of my mom and me sitting in front of the mirror. I slid it out and carefully unfolded it, ignoring the dirt rimmed edges of my nails from my scramble over the log earlier to leave the woods. I traced over my mother's face. I had to talk to her.

Crossing my fingers and closing my eyes in a silent prayer, I dialed her number.

She answered on the second ring. Immediately, like all the other times, her voice conveyed warmth, safety, and a rock-solid strength.

"Chelsea, the cell coverage is horrible. The storm is here now. Are you okay? Just say yes or no in case the phone call drops."

"I'm okay!" Then, as fast as I could, I filled her in on the events of the day.

"Chelsea Lawson! You're going to kill me one day! I knew you should have never moved there. I always had a bad feeling about Cedar Falls."

"Well, there's more. They linked me to this picture taken

over twenty years ago. To a girl named Denise. Mom, she looks just like me. I'll send you the picture."

I heard her suck in her breath, but she didn't respond.

"Mom?"

Her voice came out in a low moan. "Lord have mercy. Now?"

Goosebumps crawled up my arms as if left by invisible icy fingers. "What do you mean? Mom, you're scaring me."

Instead of answering me, I heard her sob. "Chelsea, we need to talk."

I stared at the photo of the two of us. Something flickered in the back of my mind. Something that I should have always remembered, but I still couldn't quite grasp. "Mom, why do you hate the picture of me when I was a little girl? You know, the one you threw away. Where I'm sitting next to you looking into a mirror."

"Oh, sweetie, please don't do this to me. I—" The line filled with static. And then, "Not now."

"Mom? Please...." She was keeping something from me. I had to know.

Her groan was lower, like an animal in pain. When she spoke again, it was almost to herself. "I've told so many lies, kept so many secrets. There was—"

Static interrupted her and I didn't hear the last thing she said.

"Mom? What do you mean? You're cutting out."

"There wasn't any mirror, Chelsea."

"Mom, what are you saying?"

"She wasn't a reflection. That is your little sister, Nikki."

The phone cut out again.

"Mom? Mom? I can't hear you."

"I'm —sorry. Reception here. I'll— in the city next week."

"Mom?"

It was over. My phone indicated call failure. I couldn't believe it would end this way. Did I hear her right? Did she say something about a little sister?

I dialed back immediately, only to have it go to static silence.

And just like the day when the airplane crashed, destroying the life I once knew, the world erupted around me once again. Only this time the sound wasn't a roar. This time the sound heralding destruction was soft and comforting, one I'd always relied on. This time it was my mother's voice.

The End

Turn the page for a preview of book two, Farmer in the Dead.

CHAPTER 26

Thank you for reading Mooved to Murder. The sequel continues in-

Farmer in the Dead

Trouble seems to follow Chelsea like baby ducks follow their mama. This time around, Chelsea's best friend Tilly has been accused of murdering her ex-boyfriend, Adam. When Adam's fiancé points the finger at Tilly, the police dig up a secret motivation that make things look really bad for Tilly.. and she has no alibi.

There has to be a way to clear her friend, but Chelsea is running out of ideas.

Meanwhile, Chelsea is chasing her own demons as a mystery surrounding her family comes to light. The more she learns about her past, the less sure she is of the future. Has everything in her life been a lie?

Here are more series by CeeCee James.

The Flamingo Realty Mysteries— Meet Stella O'Neil, retired FBI agent Oscar O'Neil's granddaughter. She's got a lot on her plate, trying to figure out her crazy, stubborn family, the hidden secrets that caused her grandfather's estrangement from her dad, and starting out as a realtor. Throw in a dead body found in what used to be the town's "royalty" family's manor, and she's neck deep in a mystery.

Mind Your Manors

A Dead Market

Home Strange Home

Duplex Double Trouble

MidCentury Modern Murder

With Killer Views

Baker Street Mysteries— Join Georgie, amateur sleuth and historical tour guide on her spooky, crazy adventures. As a fun bonus there's free recipes included!

Cherry Pie or Die

Cookies and Scream

Crème Brûlée or Slay

Drizzle of Death

Slash in the Pan

Terror on Top

Oceanside Hotel Cozy Mysteries—Maisie runs a 5 star hotel and thought she'd seen everything. Little did she know. From haunted pirate tales to Hollywood red carpet events, she has a lot to keep her busy.

Booked For Murder

Deadly Reservation

Final Check Out

Fatal Vacancy

Suite Casualty

ANGEL LAKE COZY MYSTERIES—ELISE COMES HOME TO HER home town to lick her wounds after a nasty divorce. Together, with her best friend Lavina, they cook up some crazy mysteries.

The Sweet Taste of Murder

The Bitter Taste of Betrayal

The Sour Taste of Suspicion

The Honeyed Taste of Deception

The Tempting Taste of Danger

The Frosty Taste of Scandal

And here is Circus Cozy Mysteries— Meet Trixie, the World's Smallest Lady Godiva. She may be small but she's learning she has a lion's heart.

Cirque de Slay

Big Top Treachery

Made in the USA
Middletown, DE
14 July 2020

12682271R00123